TONE-BONE

A COSMIC HORROR NOVEL

KYLE WINKLER

ALSO BY KYLE WINKLER

The Nothing That Is
OH PAIN
Boris Says the Words
Grasshands

"Nazis. I hate these guys."
—Indiana Jones

counterfactual (adj): relating to or expressing what has not happened or is not the case

ESCAPE FROM FUCK MOUNTAIN

Antonia Boniface fled her father on his own motorcycle. But he didn't go after her. Which bothered her at first. For about a county or two. Then she didn't mind. She knew her father was unable to keep her. Some people are uncageable. They resist bars, locks, keys. Embraces.

She could fix the bike if necessary. A 1928 Indian 101 Scout. A bike one year older than herself. It was a bike her father treated with as much love as his daughter. He'd be sore about losing the motorcycle. About losing her. She did it anyway. She was tall for her age and could get away with more than an average twelve-year-old. The United States was a year into the war with Germany and Japan. Her father would, she assumed, end up in the Army not much longer after she left. He likely died in France. She figured this much later. (In fact, he died in Belgium.) She didn't do much research. But she learned enough through the years to have a sense of where his bones moldered.

After stealing the bike, her journey went like this: alleyway to flophouse to a few broken foster homes before she told society to *fuck off*. That decision came easy. All it took for her to realize this was experiencing the same routine evil that happened to women everywhere. A handsy man. A violent drunk on a bus. The rampant negligence of society. The blind eyes of other women.

The first person she killed was another boy her age. Fourteen going on fifteen. Working in the summer, detasseling corn, laboring on farms, slopping hogs. Raking hay. Grunt stuff. With the men gone at war, everyone had to step up.

The boy'd been eyeing her from under his wide hat brim for weeks. He'd pare his nails in the shade with a penknife he kept in his overalls' bib pocket. He'd slurp peach juice off his thumb during the lunch break. He smelled of overripe fruit and moist dirt. Manure.

She kept her fists clenched in the heat of that summer. All the time. One day, she found a rusty nail. She carried it on her all the time then. She clutched it, poised between her fingers like a claw. Always prepared. So much so that her skin stained to orange just along the palm there.

Then at the end of a languid and oppressive July day, as they headed to a side barn to clean up at the water pump, they were alone in the dusk. The farm foreman had disappeared. As if by design. As if by some dark agreement.

She could feel the boy behind her. Like the flaps of a box closing. His brackish smell.

The boy clubbed her over the head with a wrench. She fell but didn't pass out. Lights in her eyes. Hot blood down her scalp and neck. The smell of rusty nails on her hands. She swelled inside. Those constant fists.

He jumped forward to try and yank her dungarees down, but Antonia pushed herself into his knees. He fell. The wrench clanked on the packed dirt. She could feel the remnant of his hand on her ass. She reached for the wrench but the boy squeezed her neck. Closing off her air. He'd have her dead if not at all. The wrench flew up and glanced her mouth. A front tooth chipped.

The wrench was out of reach. She scraped up dirt. It was her only play. Use the earth against him. She was unable to breathe and chucked it into his face. One hand came loose. She grabbed it and pulled it backwards until his fingernails touched the top of his wrist. He released her neck.

Then it was her turn.

She brought a fist down onto his Adam's apple. He gurked. He could barely see now and was breathing poorly. Still struggling. Trying to smile at her, to look into her eyes. To capture her attention. This dumb teenager trying to pretend at cowboying. She slid her hand down into his front pocket and opened the penknife. She scraped her thumbpad over it. Satisfied by the whet, she sunk it into the side of his neck.

As soon as her hand let go of the hilt she felt sick. Confused. His legs worked and kicked. Sharp, clean, young blood like a meager fountain leaked from the neckhole. But the blood was cold. Cellar cold. She jumped as if electrocuted. The boy died with that embattled smile on his face. Antonia vomited by the water pump. Washed her mouth out. Began dry heaving. Weeping.

This was the first time something felt like it was paying attention to her. Something large and necropotent.

But some people are uncageble. They resist bars, locks, keys. Embraces.

They resist people.

Humans.

Society.

Antonia Boniface fled. Again. And it was situation after similar fucking situation. After a while, the vomiting stopped. The shock wore off. But never the pain. The pain of killing hurt. It lingered. She could costume it like an actor, but she knew it was fake.

Every situation like this she imagined as a literal obstacle called Fuck Mountain. And every time this shit happened, and someone tried to manhandle her or abuse her and end her life, she was on it. At the peak. And it was escape time.

Escape from Fuck Mountain. All over again. Like a goddamn amphetamine nightmare.

For a long time, wherever that farm boy's blood had touched her hands, Antonia felt as if they were plunged into frigid water. Nothing could warm them. Ever. Nothing. She grew tall and hard. And she grew fast. The bike straddled between her legs and vibrating like a Jurassic scream. The only thing that changed her and prepped her was given to her by a woman in her first motorcycle club, Hellmother. She claimed to know magick. Hellmother gave her a new name. A name that would divorce her from her former life.

Tone-Bone.

Overnight, she became a nomad, a self-sustaining creature on two wheels. Became engines, masochism, the teachings of

Aleister Crowley, ophitic Gnosticism, talking to the Headless One, getting inked with a heartsnake. Sliding upon the earth like a malformed but free being. In Cody, Wyoming, in the valleys of darkness, she scissored her hair short in those restrained days of womanhood and lowered her voice and pulled a hat over her eyes. Made money forking hay, shoveling ditches, and working by fortnight on farms all over. There were no farm boys to threaten her. And the men back from war were hurt and tired. She ate meals alone. Slept under the stars in a ratty bedroll. At eighteen, she wrecked the Scout and stole a motorcycle outside a bar in Billings, and then she left the north and found a motorcycle club called The Wrecking Crew. Mostly men with a few women. She used them to coast across the Midwest through towns that flashed by like phosphorus in a tin pan: Bird City, Funk, Tonganoxie, Knob Noster, Eldorado, Verne. When The Wrecking Crew robbed a bank in Paoli, Indiana, she split. She hit Ft. Wayne, Detroit, Peoria, and then a long push toward Alaska. She rode north into the cold wastes of Canada and dodged the roaming eyeball of the lower forty-eight states and the larger world. On the way, she slept in open fields or crawled through unlatched motel windows and then into vacant beds. She slept on the leeside of haybales. Tone-Bone collected what people left behind. Like a poor farmer in the old days of gleaning wheat from fields. A creased paperback of Dumas's *The Count of Monte Cristo*, mail-ordered pamphlets on astrology, Egyptology, and occult practices in medieval France. In Fairbanks, she gained swollen knuckles, glass embedded under the skin, a permanently broken toe, and a keloid scar on her hipbone. All this by twenty-five. She returned to the Midwest and worked off the books repairing motorcycles for booze and food in towns that no one bothered to move out of. She seduced a few war widows and confirmed her preference for women over men. Townsfolk whispered about her as *that one strange woman*. She lived in a different world while the pert housewives drove past her in their wide dresses and blonde curls. She saved money and deposited strategically in banks across Iowa, Minnesota, Illinois. The hippies carved a space for her to trail, though she hated them. She spent every birthday through her forties in solitude like a beacon atop a skyscraper. She listened as heavy rock melted into disco and burned into punk. The actor beat the farmer for president. Reality flip-flopped.

She began to walk with a bow in her legs. Had plantar fasciitis. Lost some teeth to cavities.

Four gangs, three stints in county lockups, and many lovers later, she found a small group of likeminded biker terrors, all women, headquartered in a three-story farmhouse in rural southwestern Indiana, and there they had more freedom, more ability to do what they wanted when they wanted, to abandon responsibility in the morning like a child in a hot car and parse the asphalt under their wheels as if it was a finger tracing the bumps on a book of Braille. They were The Fuck Offs. Tone-Bone's face reddened with windburn, chapped and peeling; her skin toughened. She pierced her left ear with a rusty safety pin and put a gold hoop through it.

Then it was 1982 and she was fifty-three years old.

And in that year, Tone-Bone killed a Nazi.

Not a skinhead. Not a casual fascist. No. A true-blue swastika-swallowing Nazi piece of shit. Tone-Bone had seen *The Boys from Brazil* a few years back in the theatre. It left a nasty taste on her memory-tongue. She also remembered why her father was eventually taken from her the year she fled him on his own motorcycle and she remembered reading in the newspaper the words NAZIS INVADE and JAPAN ATTACKS and AXIS POWERS and they tattooed her conscience like angry neon.

NAZI DOG FOOD

This Nazi had worked as a guard at Bergen-Belsen. He'd taken leave to visit a sick family member a few months before the U.S. liberated the camp in 1945. Before the joes came in and had to bulldoze bodies into mass graves and feed starving people rice gloop to keep them nourished. The Nazi fell into luck. The luckiest fascist ever. The Nazi kept a low profile after Berlin fell. He forged papers. He dodged the Allies and weaseled his way to Mexico on a steamer carrying refugees. And then, eventually—he snaked into middle America.

By 1980, he'd felt safe and charmed his way into local white nationalist groups in southern Indiana. These ideological amoebas would meet way out on farms in the deep woods where people couldn't hear them sing racist anthems and cheer on dog fights in pole barns and drink until the rangy guitar music faded. The old Nazi guard was big shit in that scene. The Americans practically sat at his feet and lapped up his moldy memories of bodies and death. Gullible children. What was it with them and disaster? Christ.

Often, Tone-Bone showed up at these deep rural gatherings for the music. She liked punk. Loved it. Her gang made a business of hosting punk shows to make money. Other times they acted as muscle for punk shows in cities like Indianapolis, Chicago, Detroit, Cleveland, and Pittsburgh. That night, Tone-Bone was muscle. Along with a few other Fuck Offs strategically placed around the grounds. They got hired more than male motorcycle clubs because, the theory goes, no one would expect to get their ass served to them by a pack of feral women. Which was true. The women may not have been able to hit harder but they did considerably more damage when called upon to do so. Also, the white nationalists possessed good drugs and decent booze and they gave them both to her for free. So she partook. She tolerated their inanity for the trip.

Let it be known that Tone-Bone started off as an opportunist. Yes.

She didn't end this way, though. That took a while.

The Nazi's name was Meise. He wasn't suave. But he was confident. And he smoked these horrible cigarettes. They smelled like a chemical fire near a cow pen. Meise lit a new one with a slim expensive lighter that was black with a silver SS death's head on it. They both stood some distance apart under the stars while drunk people shambled and collapsed around them.

He asked if Tone-Bone smoked. She said she'd rather drink cat urine. He chuckled. She hated chuckling. No one should chuckle. Not even small children in fantasy stories.

Especially not children in fantasy stories.

She drank her beer and waited for the drugs to smooth her hate when the Nazi started reminiscing. Two skinheads circled around in their Doc Martens, khakis, and flight jackets. They wanted to be wowed. The Nazi laid it on.

But he slipped up. He said too much. He wasn't merely a Good German who'd attended rallies. No. He mentioned Belsen. The piles of bodies. His luck at getting out before the camps were closed, etc. He realized this slip and side-glanced at Tone-Bone. She didn't smile. He whispered to the young worshipping skinheads. They looked at her. The men traded brief hand gestures. Then they returned to the melee in the pole barn.

Up to this point, Tone-Bone didn't think much of the guy other than he was a prick with an accent.

But now he knew that she knew he was a legit-shit Nazi. Most people in their circles wouldn't have cared. But some reflex across her face told Meise that she would like to stomp him into burger.

And what would a clandestine war criminal like him do to stop her—a leather-clad stranger who didn't appreciate his advances—from telling the world? The skinheads were one thing. But the muscle and other gangs and clubs didn't always gibe with every ideology. Opportunism was the default mode. They worked on a brutal trade system. X for Y. No love lost.

She figured the young skinheads were rounding up fellow shaved goons to get the message across to her. Probably with a knife between the ribs. They also made snide remarks about her café racer. The Honda CB750. She didn't care. Hanging off the monkey bars on a Harley Davidson was for the birds.

No one ever jacked with the muscle at a show, racists or otherwise, woman or man, but she wasn't taking chances. Tone-

Bone wanted to head this particular stagecoach off at the pass.

She offered the old Nazi an invitation to meet at the Golden Forest cemetery. Lots of culverts and hills. Wild turkeys strutting among the gravestones. It was dark, secret. It was her speed. The Nazi wanted to fuck. He was old, isolated. The southern Indiana girls took a shine to him but didn't want his cock.

Tone-Bone figured his plan was to have her killed. But he relented and softened when she extended an invitation.

In turn she wanted to kill him. She was older and tired. But she had to do it. To settle something that rattled around too much in the memory.

Two hours later. The night was cloudy. Thick. Usually the gravestones glowed with moonlight. He came alone. He must've lost his paranoid streak. I mean, look at her. She was decked in leather from the waist up, denim from the waist down. Her shirt said *Fuck you* and her salty hair hung down by her chin like strands from an abandoned bird's nest.

He was smoking one of those disgusting cigarettes. He meandered through the stones. A large trench coat settled over his shoulders. What a dipshit. Or maybe she was the moron. She had her guard down. She scanned the cemetery, and she couldn't see much. She'd have heard someone sneaking up from a ways off anyhow. Maybe.

He stood a few yards apart, stinking up the air. He tilted his head at an open grave.

"We are to proceed our activities there, eh?"

She shook her head.

He pointed his cig at her hands. He cupped the smoke like an old movie star. But something past his head in the distance caught her eye. A reflection. She motioned that way. Friends of yours, she said. He sighed, nodding as if his aspirations for subterfuge weren't fruitless against a brain like hers.

He lifted his hand up in a signal.

Two 4x4 swamp trucks with light racks on top cranked over. The lights were blinding even from that distance. Tone-Bone flipped them off. The trucks backed up and took off.

"How do I know there aren't any other of your friends waiting around?"

"You will have to trust me." Then his eyes widened with an idea. "Here. Take my cigarette."

Those were precious to him. Even she knew that, and she knew nothing about him. She wondered what he knew about her. Something about him smelled off. And it wasn't foreign cigarettes. It was a corrupted stench. Like decaying meat in the jaws of a lion.

He stepped forward and extended the smoke. It burned like a fuse. The only glowing star in the dark.

She took it and inhaled. The filter had his saliva on it. It was worse than the taste of smoke.

"You have dirt on your hands," he said.

"Because I was digging your grave."

She had no time to respond. He was fast. Surprisingly fast. He leapt across the grave and tackled her. The cig fell onto the dirt. He had the advantage of height and toppled her but as she landed on her back she put her right foot into his chest. Barely. She tried to get her hands up near her boot. He thought she wanted to choke him. Meise grabbed her wrists and pulled himself closer to her, not seeming to suffer the pain of her boot. There was a small gun in a holster on the lower part of her shin. Usually it was a knife. She changed it the week before for no reason whatsoever.

As she struggled with him inches from her face she did not hear him gasp or breathe deeply. His attack was silent and in his open mouth was a pit and in that pit even for a flash she believed she glimpsed lights flashing.

She wrenched her wrist free away and pulled the trigger. The bullet tore into Meise's stomach. He rolled to his knees as if in lopsided prayer then fell backward and she heard his ligaments pop as he did. Then she kicked him to his back and pinned her knees on his ribcage and cut off his thumbs.

One-two.

Fuckem, she thought. Fuck that thumb.

*Aaaa*nd fuck that thumb.

She planned to feed the thumbs to Meise's dog. He bragged about that dog at the punk show. Dog this. Dog that.

Up to this point, Tone-Bone had killed ten people in her life. Meise would've made eleven. It was a good number. She liked that number. Eleven was two poles. Two knives. She'd get a tattoo of the number soon. Maybe in an empty spot on a shoulder blade. Not because she was proud. She wasn't a cold-blooded murderer. She viewed it as revenge.

And killing a Nazi wasn't murder per se.

C'mon. That was justice. Dare we say it was even a certain species of justice for a pessimistic anarchistic cynic like Tone-Bone.

All of the ten previous people tried to kill Tone-Bone first in an overly enthusiastic and ravenous way. It's not worth going into all the details here, suffice it to say that all of them (men and women) had either tried to rape, maim, or kill her. So she killed them first. Nowhere near as noble as one would hope, but there it was.

She often thought tragedy didn't have to make you a messed-up person, but it sure helped.

The Nazi whispered through blood bubbles and agony that he thought they were going to have sex. On a gravestone. He laughed. As if he deserved it somehow. Like tricking him was a shameful act. She knelt harder down in his face, holding the gun on him.

He said: "Ironic, no, that you're doing to me what you so claim is vile about *Nationalsozialismus?*"

"Don't be an instigator. You killed people because of who they are. I kill because people try to stop me from being who I am. There's a difference."

"You lied about our...engagement."

Blood glazed his lips. He choked on his own fluids. She'd shot him through the lower lobe of his lung. Probably had collapsed. Immense pain. Good.

"Yeah," she said. "I prefer women. So."

"*Der Muschi.*" He spread his fingers in front of his mouth. Too weak to stick his tongue all the way out. "*Ja. Es passt zu einer Hure wie dir.*"

"I assume you're complimenting me. I do give good head. *Danke.*"

The Nazi smiled then coughed black liquid. Deep dirty lung blood. An oil slick down his dress shirt and blazer. She felt a mist of it on her face. She stood. She dug the toe of her boot into the bullet wound. He wailed weakly. Then she wiped the boot toe in the grass. A stray dog would come along later and sniff and lick at the blood.

Goddamn.

It was so easy to hate a Nazi. Really, it was, Tone thought. But she hoped it wouldn't get any harder.

Here's the thing.

Tone-Bone hated people. Full-stop. But she didn't want to eradicate a group of people because they had a different religion or hair color or whatever. She hated life, generally. Broadly. She had such high disdain for evolved intelligence in the form of *Homo sapiens* that the brain and the cerebral cortex was more of an affront to her everyday existence than any individual act of cruelty. And yet, she hated cruelty.

What could she do? She was a complicated person.

Anyway. After Meise died, she dragged the corpse to a fresh grave the cemetery's sextons had prepared earlier that day. A fresh grave she'd jumped down into and dug a few feet deeper earlier that night. It was a trick she'd learned from an old EC Comics title she found in one of those empty motel rooms from her youth. Maybe *The Haunt of Fear*. Ah, the self-education of a vagabond and a gleaner.

Tone-Bone snagged the dead man's wallet and house keys.

Then she kicked the Nazi and he collapsed into the grave, a jumble of blood-limbs and death-wheeze. It was not as delicious a revenge as she suspected it would be. Maybe he needed the fascist get-up, all that black cloth and white trim and snazzy silver jewelry. Or did he need to say those magic evil words and give the salute. Who knows.

She couldn't care less.

She let herself into his house with his keys not too far away. A well-groomed terrier barked when she entered.

"Shut up."

The dog whimpered.

Tone-Bone opened a can of Alpo with the Bowie knife she used on the Nazi. She sniffed the food. She dumped it into a soup pan. She dropped the severed thumbs on top. The terrier ravaged the whole mess. Then it spent a little time gnawing on the thumb bones.

She searched the cupboards. Tipping out what little the Nazi fed himself on. Lots of his shitty cigarettes were stacked in the corners. But there was a box of macaroni and cheese. She boiled the pasta and mixed the cheese powder. She kicked her boots up onto the kitchen table and ate the food. The terrier begged for scraps. She scraped them onto the floor. Then she released the dog into the wild.

That was tough. She liked dogs. She'd always befriended them. The terrier wouldn't last long, she figured. But it deserved a romp before a final back-alley duel with a cur.

Tone-Bone thought about pilfering and fencing some items in the house but instead lit a kerosene lamp. She shut all the windows. Locked them. Toweled in the leaky spots. Turned on the gas range.

She waited to hear the hiss. She waited for the tangy smell.

Then she left.

She was shifting into high gear some ways down the road when the Nazi's house exploded behind her. Rattled her spine. Shook her hips. It felt good.

MENOPAUSE EATS YOUTH

Tone-Bone didn't own a house. She did not have one single place to lay her head. Instead the Fuck Offs used a network of trailers along the river north of town. It was one of many bug-out shelters. Illegal, off-the-grid, stone age basic. Depended on where people were in their daily sobriety or sexual hookups. Some hours before sunrise, the closest trailer was empty. She needed to fumigate the smell of Nazi cigarettes from her clothes, her hair, her skin.

She pulled up to her bunk for the day. She threw a canvas tarp over her bike.

Then she stopped.

She heard noises. Rippling river over the berm. The tarp ruffling. Her own breath. Something in the air wobbled.

Maybe a metal clang. Like a window cranking open or closed.

There was a familiar whistle in her ears. A warning. A lightness in the skeleton. But not a tingle. She never got tingles.

Tone-Bone was exhausted and planned to fall into the busted couch as soon as she could with a bottle of whiskey.

So she knew there was a problem when she stepped inside. The couch was shifted. The lights were off. The Fuck Offs never cleaned or moved or did anything. Lights always stayed on, hooked up to car batteries underneath the floor.

Heaviness crashed into her shoulders. She tripped forward. She smelled men and their hot alcoholic breath. Those two skinheads from the punk show. The white nationalist lackeys. They meant to hit her in the head but struck her shoulder blade. Which hurt like a sonofabitch. Tone-Bone fell to a knee. One booted her in the ribcage from the left. All air exited her body.

She wondered if this was always the plan. Meise would hustle her and then let her get bagged by two assholes. Did that mean they knew she killed their buddy? Were they tracking her? The trailer wasn't a secret.

Tone-Bone didn't have a weapon on her now except the Bowie knife. She'd tossed the gun down the road after blowing up the house.

With late middle-aged stiffness working against their young drunkenness, she leapt for the couch. Like a broken frog. One of the men struck the floor with whatever metal pole he wielded. The second hit the heel of her boot. She grabbed a cushion from the couch and charged the biggest one. She felt the pole's strike *whuff* into the cushion. The big skinhead collapsed over the kitchen four-top and onto the floor. Glass ashtrays, dirty plates, steak knives. All exploding and crashing. The fridge door popped open. A parallelogram of light spread awkwardly over the trailer's interior.

She could sense waves of embarrassment. A menopausal woman was beating their asses. In a leather jacket. Lightly drunk.

Well, they didn't want the victory enough. Testosterone only goes so far.

Tone-Bone turned with the cushion and shoved it into the second skinhead's face. He had a short-bladed knife. She heard it *shink-shuff* into the pillow material. She angled her body and ran the second guy back onto the couch. She flipped the light switch by the door. The lights didn't come on. These kids couldn't have been more than nineteen or twenty years old.

She pulled the knife from her boot. The bigger guy was now standing in the kitchen.

"Your Hitler Jesus is dead, boys," she said. "I shot him."

They did not react to this news.

The one on the couch said, out of breath, "He can't die." He laughed wildly, his attitude about this was cocksure.

She was taller than both of them. And they were nervous now. Unsure of their abilities. She shocked them. And, really, they hadn't come with any effective weapon. Just a random sawed-off pole. They had to be new and this was their initiation or a test.

Tone-Bone swiped at the couch skinhead. She wondered whether she had control or if they did and were just done playing. The kid she pushed over the table was squirting lighter fluid that he'd stowed in his jacket. Painting the inside of her half of the trailer. He flicked open a Zippo and tossed it behind her as he leapt out the door. As she watched this, the kid on the couch sneaked past her and jumped across the spreading flame. They stood outside there like guardians to a subterranean portal. The fire was hesitant but urged on after a moment. The only moment Tone had to think with. The skinheads still held the pipes at the ready. There was one functional door. The blocked one. The other at the opposite end of the trailer was boarded up. The flames ringed the doorframe now. She had under fifteen seconds to get out. Behind her on the wall were pictures from the family that lived there years before. Three by five wooden frames with glass. She snatched two. Then she flung them like a frisbee right at them. One in the neck, glancing one of them enough to distract and the other hitting the kid between the stomach and the nuts. Tone-Bone pulled her knife. She ran and lunged at them through the fire and slashed at them. She missed both and tuck and rolled. Poorly. But she was up and slicing at both fast enough that they stepped back and one of them dropped their pipe and the other pulled him along to leave.

"Get gone and don't ever fucking come here again."

"The Fuck Offs are dead, you old bitch."

They both made the same hand gestures as they had to Meise. She pointed the way out with the serrated edge. As in, *fucking skedaddle*. The skinheads jogged on around the trailer and down to the river. The sound of a small off-board motor puttered up. They drove a fishing boat to a murder job. What did that say about what they thought about her? About the Fuck Offs?

Tone-Bone left everything behind. The trailer spumed smoke and light. The heat was unbearable. She pulled the tarp off the Honda and rode to the nearest gas station. It was 3:44 a.m. The pay phone was around the side, hidden from the arc lights. Hurt to breathe. Probably bruised or broke a rib. She called another Fuck Off, Braincase.

The phone rang for a solid minute.

"What."

"It's Tone."

"I know who it is."

"The trailer got broke. Skinheads from the show followed me back. They got it out for us now. I killed Meise."

"The cigarette guy."

"Yeah."

"And?"

"Need a new cooler."

Braincase gave Tone-Bone a new address. It was a rambling set of obtuse directions to a place outside of town. Another trailer in that dilapidated network of rural outposts. "No power or water," Braincase said.

"Goddamn it."

"Doesn't matter. You need to be over here by nine. We're going to Kentucky."

Not this again, she thought.

"What? Why?"

"You know why. We're gonna go snag that priestess in Paducah."

"This is a waste of time, that girl. She's a truck stop fortune teller. She knows nothing."

Tone-Bone heard Braincase sit up in bed or wherever she was. Her voice was sexy and cruel. Attractive and repulsive. Like a rare tropical flower that bloomed divinely but smelled like death.

"Hey, you get on board with this or don't, but we're going. Better you don't hang around in town for a few days anyway."

Braincase hung up. Bugs swarmed in the arc light. It's all Tone-Bone heard. Smelled like taco meat outside. And gas fumes and gutter dirt. She bought a candy bar in the gas station where the teenaged attendant stared at her like an escaped wolf and she ate the sugar leaning against the bike. The heavy blanket feeling of something paying attention to her returned. A vast necropotent gaze.

This girl in Kentucky would be the ruination of them all. And while Braincase and the other Fuck Offs wanted that to some degree, Tone-Bone found it lacking. They'd met the girl while hosting punk shows. The girl partied. Slept around with some of the gang. But then she started spouting weird witchy shit. Doing astrological charts for Braincase, Thorn, Poxy, Tasker, and others. Made no sense. But the women were obsessed. Fawning over this scrawny, scurvied Girl from Paducah. They didn't even know her real name. The girl had her own tarot deck. Handmade, hand drawn. She read fortunes. She shuffled cards with titles like the Broken Babysitter, the Yawning Dog, the Black Cancer, and the Six of Shits.

Tone-Bone had been able to avoid her up to now. But it seemed inevitable she'd have to go. And it was true. She couldn't be around for a while. The skinheads knew where to find her. She'd have to duck out of state for a bit.

The last reading the Paducah Priestess gave for Braincase went like this: there was a god, of a sort, far in the erasure of blackest space that wants to inhabit the Fuck Offs. But they have work to do to bring it earthward. If they do, life will uncouple from the living. The more suicidal of the group seized on this. And that was all it took.

But Tone-Bone, while sympathetic to the message, thought it was bullshit. And, moreover, should this Paducah girl be right, nothing good could come of it. Or nothing bad.

Nothing at all.

CRAWL OVER THE OHIO

Tone-Bone didn't even end up going to the cooler Braincase told her about. She just rode around until sunrise then went to Smitty's Diner. The 24-hour place. She stared into the tabletop, her shoulders and back sore and hurting. Pain killers and aspirin helped. Endless cups of coffee. She needed the coffee mug to keep her hands warm. People stared at her. That didn't help.

She had a simple philosophy. Don't fuck with me, and I won't fuck with you. Libertarianism was bullshit. Same as utilitarianism or personal growth or whatever those positive souls who drank Sanka and obsessively watched *The Phil Donohue Show* thought. Let them screw happiness or sunshine or whatever it was into each other. Not for her.

She was a cynic. Nothing good could come from or of the world. But she wasn't suicidal. Erasing yourself didn't solve anything. It only hurt more. Which sounded like an ideology that already existed, but labels withered. Labels meant someone was pulling the strings. She lived simply inside a certain aesthetic. And it was an aesthetic that said: Get on Board with Rot. Because that's all there was: Rot and Growth.

But mostly rot.

Maybe, she thought, her motto was: Creative Decay.

Go to pot but do it with some sort of style.

Even so, she was the most "upbeat" of the Fuck Offs. For example, this one woman, Thorn. She used to be a kindergarten teacher. She was the darkest of them. No one asked her what changed her. They didn't care. But Tone-Bone did. Sort of. Turns out that one day Thorn suddenly sighted an irretrievable horror in the eyes of her students, those kids, making crafts with Elmer's glue and colored construction paper. She saw enough to drive her to hell. She walked right out of the classroom. Never returned. Joined the Fuck Offs a week later.

Tone-Bone figured that was Thorn's version of the farm boy's cold blood. Every member had a cursed talisman like it.

She met up with the gang. They were the equivalent of the living dead wearing sunglasses and leather. Piercings, tats, long sinuous scars and sharp tongues. They were off. Riding in the morning mist south with a heavy cloud cover. Taking backroads, never the interstates. They stuck close to the Wabash River and how it steamed in the dawn like a separate gargantuan animal, exhaling smoke. They zoomed through places like Cave-In-Rock, Humm Wye, and Golconda.

No one asked about Tone's injuries, her condition. No one asked about the skinheads. No one asked about the punk show or the immolated trailer.

Comfort was for the rest of the world.

Not for them.

They found the priestess in a trailer park in a double-wide, presumably her own, doing a reading for a young mother with curlers in her hair, who wore a nightdress with stained armpits. Braincase and Tone-Bone were invited to sit at the table and watch. The mother didn't mind. The priestess was calm as curdled milk. And barefoot. She'd never seen the priestess wear shoes. Ever. As if the solid earth was a battery that recharged her or spoke directly through her soles. The other members waited outside and smoked or watched stray dogs take a shit on the gravel road.

The priestess had laid out four long Tarot cards. She was flipping another over. It was called The Anti-Death. Pictured on it was a long punishing line of people walking into a massive house-sized birthday cake. The mother-in-nightdress was confused and upset.

"Someone will return to you," the priestess said, giddy. Her eyes were dark and sunken like treasure thrown overboard from a pirate galleon.

"But I haven't lost anyone."

"Oh, it's not anyone from this life."

The mother shifted uneasily in her seat. The priestess turned over another card.

The Green Star. Seemed innocuous to Tone-Bone. But the priestess made a small gasp. She mussed the order of the cards as if to disturb them, as if they were mounting an attack upon her. She stood up.

"We're through. You'll have to leave."

"Hey! Where's my fortune? You said you'd tell my future."

The priestess gathered the cards. "You don't have one," she said. "Get out."

Braincase stood and led the woman out who held herself as if she was her own baby. Then the biker took the empty seat.

"What's the Green Star?" Braincase asked.

"You wouldn't ask if you knew. It's a new card. Made it this morning. I shouldn't have done it." The priestess seemed nervous. Scared, even. "I've done seven readings today. Every single one included that card. Even if I didn't have it in the deck."

Braincase turned to Tone-Bone to show the probity of the statement, but Tone shook her head.

But then the priestess tried to turn her fear into eagerness. A demeanor change. Like a cowering dog spontaneously overcome with deep revenge.

"You decided then? You want to know."

Braincase said they did. All of them did. They wanted to know. The priestess demanded time then. Every Fuck Off would need a thorough reading. Some would take a whole day. And they would need their astrological charts filled out in full. Braincase tapped the heel of her boot on the linoleum. Tone-Bone didn't follow Braincase. No one Fuck Off was a leader per se. But some of them pulled the others in more directions more often. This whole trip was an obsession that Braincase was sowing into the others. Except Tone-Bone. Astrology, she thought, was for idiots who didn't have the initiative to give their life direction through sheer will. It was, like many other made-up stories, yet another distraction from getting shit done. Like Nazism. Or most political ideologies, for that matter.

The priestess had a strangely shaved head, like it was strategically shaved, and the top was kept long. She wore multiple pewter rings on each finger and her entire neck was tattooed with a solid spiraling black line. She wasn't pleasant to look at, not by a stretch, but she did have those deep-set eyes, large and wide, that hid in a purplish shadow. Again, Tone-Bone found that some people's physical attributes stood in for what passed as actual substance. Big tits meant attraction or sexual knowledge. Clean, straight teeth meant honesty. Big eyes meant wisdom. Whatever. People were simpletons. Those types of details never panned out.

Braincase wanted her fortune and astrology chart done first. So everyone else had to go kick rocks for a couple of hours. Thorn, Poxy, Tasker, and Nonsense went to eat. Hopeless guarded the priestess's trailer. Tone-Bone bought a six pack from a gas station and drank it by the river. Her body ached. Her guts moaned. Even her fingernails shivered in their nailbeds. The Ohio River flowed like a poison snake made of brown waste.

Not far in the wavelets that lapped onto the shore, a foul-smelling foam wiggled in the breeze and a fast-food restaurant bag sailed on top. A Fishbeard's Feast paper bag once full of fried crap but now translucent with fat.

She drank a few and lost herself in the flowing water. But a noise swelled. She looked up and across to the far bank. It was almost like a metallic panting. Like an exhausted and dying road construction machine. She couldn't tell where it was coming from. Could've been a factory. But when she stood, a massive river barge floated into view. It was slowing and coming to a stop. It was sixty yards away. Piled with trash. Something about the immensity of that much crap impressed her.

The top of the pile broke open. As if a bird was burrowed underneath. But it wasn't a bird. Refuse and cans and plastic spilled down. Some fell into the river. It was a hand pushing through the trash. Then another. Tone-Bone stood. The panting sound was coming from the barge. From underneath the shit, stood a person. They stared at Tone-Bone.

She knew who it was.

Herr Meise. The Nazi she'd shot. That she'd *killed*. That she'd killed *dead*. She crushed the beer can against her head to wake up. It hurt. Good. Maybe she'd not gotten enough sleep. Drank too early? Too many drugs? It was, she tried to convince herself, a hallucination.

Meise took a step, stumbled, and rolled down the trash heap and landed onto the river like it was a flat pane of glass. Tone-Bone didn't know what to do. Run, stay, drink?

Meise scrabbled atop the Ohio River like a water bug on all fours, defying the surface tension. He was bent and pale and moving in fits and spurts. And he was fast. Tone had her knife— had not bothered to get a new gun. But what kind of bullets would be needed for whatever this was? As soon as the new insectile Nazi had crossed half the distance to the shore and was seconds away from her—he fell into the water with an undramatic splash.

The river barge bellowed and moved on like a sad leviathan. The wake created larger lapping waves that broke at her feet where she stood as a maniac would stand on the grounds of an asylum conversing with the trees. Was what she saw real? She thought about those skinheads. What they said. *He can't die*. Those stupid hand gestures.

She was freezing. Shivering. And it was definitely not from the room temp beers.

The water near shore swirled. Bubbled. Thrashed. Below the surface something big was roiling it, like a school of febrile fish. The remaining three beers hung on the plastic ring in her hand. She'd club any fucking thing that crawled out of the water, fascist or no. Red color, like blood, now boiled in the water. She waited for a hand. A melted face. Something to emerge. But the tumult faded, still deep red.

Then a large fish leapt out in an arc like a missile and knocked Tone-Bone in the chest. She fell. The beers flung back and one broke open, spraying out foam and spinning around. The fish was two feet long and thick. Like a silver muscular arm, gyrating and slapping. Leaping on her. It pounded her head and her stomach. It rose and fell. It crushed another rib. She couldn't breathe from that. She finally bear-hugged it to her chest, but its mouth opened.

The fish had long spiny teeth. Its jaw snapped. It lunged at her. This was no fish she'd ever seen pulled from a river or a lake. She swung it away into the muddied dirt and the fish just flopped back in big bounces toward her like in a nightmare. She unsheathed the Bowie knife and crouched the same way a caveman would've faced off megafauna. When it was right in her face, fangs bared, she swiped at it and gave it a gash. Bouncing chaotically, it growled, the fishmouth foaming red like shook-up blood-beer. But it was enough.

The fish sprung backward with a leap into the Ohio. Tone-Bone collapsed onto the shore.

"What in thunderation was that." An old timer was standing behind her holding a tackle box and pole. Eyes wrinkled from the lit cigar clamped in his mouth. Mesh cap resting on his head. "You okay, lady?"

Tone-Bone stood. She was soaked. Cut. Bruised. Broken. Confused.

"I'm not a lady," she said.

He chuckled. Jesus. People and chuckling. "Sure look like a lady to me."

Tone-Bone smelled like algae scum. She opened one of the remaining beers. It spluttered over. She downed the whole thing and belched. The old timer pulled a face like he wanted to take back what he'd said.

"You ever seen a fish like that?" she asked. "Fucking fangs like a viper."

The old timer shook his head.

"Never in my 85 years."

"Thought so."

The old timer reconsidered fishing.

Tone-Bone handed the remaining beer to him and revved the motorcycle and headed back to the priestess's trailer. She was done with Paducah, Kentucky.

TWO HALVES
OF THE ORANGE

Last one up. Tone-Bone's turn for a reading.

"Is this necessary?" she said.

"Sit the goddamn down," Braincase said. The other five Fuck Offs were in the living room, tearing a Bible apart page by page. Poxy had taken one of the onion skin pages and used it as a rolling paper for a massive joint. They proceeded to pass it around.

Tone-Bone pulled Braincase aside.

"What is this adding to our goal? This feels like a giant sidestep. We should be moving on. Riding. Trying to push the Dragons and Motormouths out." There were many motorcycle clubs or gangs, but the two biggest competitors for fun, drugs, and money were the Dragons and the Motormouths.

Braincase took a deep hit off the joint. Held it. Tried not to cough. Then blew the exhaust into Tone-Bone's face.

"That bitch said she can uncouple life from the living. Doesn't that pop your cherry, Toney-Baloney?"

She'd had calming visions of living alone on Earth. Being the sole proprietor. Empty streets. Quiet rooms.

"How?" Tone-Bone said.

"Get the reading. That's how."

Fuuuck.

The priestess patted the kitchen chair next to her.

"C'mon. I ain't bite you hard then. Just a nibble. The rest of y'all need to shoo. I can't do no reading with y'all smoking me out. Beat it."

The women filed out. Bikes roared. Off they went.

Tone-Bone was alone with the priestess. They sat in silence for five minutes, the priestess waiting the hard-ass biker out. But Tone-Bone was well-schooled in the discipline of shutting up and staying shut up. It was a second nature. The kitchen counters was lined with different Ball jars steeping various leaves, grasses, dried herbs. A cage by the window had some parakeets and small colorful birds flapping about. Incense burned. The priestess was barefoot. She must've bit her toenails. They were nubbins. But her fingers were pristine. Gorgeous. Tone-Bone was thinking that she could fuck this woman—under the right circumstances.

"I don't want no reading," she said.

"That's not a nice thing to say to your hostess."

"We're not staying."

"Says who?"

"Me."

"Oh, you're the leader?"

"No, we don't have one."

"Well, that seems complicated."

"For idiots, it is."

The priestess put the cards down.

"Fine. Go on. Leave. I ain't gonna stop you."

Tone-Bone pushed back the chair and left. The birds in the cage erupted inside. She straddled the Honda and turned the bike over, but everything went silent. She couldn't hear the birds. Or the noises outside. Kids running. A muffler-less car driving by. "Hey," she said. "What the shit." She could hear herself, her voice but not the world. Why is this happening now, she thought. She was having a stroke? Or did her eardrums burst?

Tone-Bone turned around. The priestess stood in the trailer's doorway observing the mute and speechless world.

The priestess was talking and gesticulating but nothing came out of her mouth. She couldn't tell what strange envelope she'd slid into. Tone turned the bike over again. It throbbed between her legs. The bike felt soft. It felt squishy. She had to squeeze it to balance it. Something dropped off the front frame and onto her boot toe.

Blood. Blood seeped out of the engine's dissipation fins. The bike rumbled again. What looked like blood oozed from the exhaust pipes and burbled from under the gas tank cap. "Come the fuck on." She killed the ignition and swung a leg off and shouldered past the priestess. She grabbed the chair and sat down again.

Sounds returned immediately when her ass touched the vinyl seat. Like plugging in a stereo cord. The priestess made a motion as if to ask for permission to sit at her own table.

Tone-Bone relented.

"That silence shit? Blood in the engine? My bike? Don't ever do that to me again."

"I didn't do anything, sweetie."

Toothy smile.

"Then who did?"

The priestess dealt the cards. "Well, let's see."

Her reading was long but thorough. Tone-Bone had to drink five different liquids from the jars on the counter. None tasted bad or made her gag. But none tasted good. Mostly what she imagined licking a tree or dirt would be like. At one point, Tone-Bone had to put a canvas bag over her head. She wasn't keen on that crap.

In the end, the priestess came to two concrete conclusions.

First, that Tone-Bone would live a long time, but not as herself (which made no sense).

Second, that from here on until the end, she'd have no peace. (Tone-Bone thought of the old Nazi scampering across the water…seemed rather accurate.) Because, the priestess added, she was the one who was allowed to pluck the orange.

"Peace is overrated," Tone-Bone said. "Wait—what orange?"

"Go over to that closet in the hall. Open the door."

Tone-Bone considered this…girl, for that was what she was. Truly. A young woman. Maybe she was legal to drink. Maybe she was college age. She definitely was the right age to be someone's wayward daughter. If she was to trust this girl—and the reality of that was shifting—what could she expect behind that door? It was a demented version of Bozo the Clown's Grand Prize Game. Tone-Bone stood before the door and listened. Nothing. She tapped the handle, as if it could be hot or would electrocute her.

She opened the door. It was a normal hall closet, appropriate for a trailer. Small, dark, cramped. Except, growing from out of the floor was an orange tree. Bright green leaves. The tree's skin was healthy. And there, in the middle, hanging like a fat bright teardrop, was a ripe orange.

"That grew overnight last week. It wanted to show me something," the priestess said from behind.

"Who did?"

"Take the orange."

"Or what?"

"Pick it, Antonia. Bring it here."

Tone-Bone spun as if she'd been knifed.

"How do you know that name?"

The priestess looked bored. She waved the biker's anger away. Then she was slightly offended. She was a priestess after all. "C'mon. Pick it. You're wasting time."

Tone-Bone pulled the orange off the tree. She didn't want to. She actively told herself not to do it, but there was her hand. It was moving out from her. Grasping the fruit. Pulling downward. The satisfying *snap* of the stem cracking off the top. The orange felt good in her hand, but she was glad to give it over to the priestess.

Her host hefted it in her palm and talked to it.

The priestess spun a hypnotic story about a god who was born and trapped in a star and who has teeth on teeth and suns in its lungs and all this la-di-da mumbo jumbo shit that gave Tone-Bone the fantods. It was, yes, of course, an interdimensional being that chronologically ate you backwards—it erased you from space-time history by consuming and eradicating everything you own/touch/interact with. What a score for the Fuck Offs who were so incredibly poised to stop all life through the most complete means. Not genocide, not murder. Not even anti-natalism. A declining birth rate wouldn't solve the issue. One life was too many. The point was to erase existence from existence. A self-swallowing mouth, to be exact.

The priestess continued, bringing the orange closer to her lips.

"And it wants to visit, this being. It wants so much to subsume and swallow us. Do not think of it as evil, she said. 'Cause evil is just a point of view. Is a volcano evil because it explodes and covers a village in lava? No. A volcano is just doing what volcanos do. But we must continue our readings. And the stars! So much to observe and record in the stars. We'll need telescopes."

So, that's what Braincase wanted. This was why the Fuck Offs were in Paducah. Not for the priestess, really. But for the star god. Whatever that was. Braincase and the others had the hard-on for *uncoupling life from the living*. This was exactly the method by which they'd take it all down.

Well, there's your ticket.

The whole time the priestess spoke about the being, she spun the orange like a planet in her hands. She cried. Thankful, grateful. She was chosen. Or, she merely reached out, and it responded.

Like, how does that happen? Tone-Bone wondered. How does something like that even begin to occur?

Tone-Bone didn't get an answer. She figured it had something to do with the cards and the drugs. Maybe the whole galaxy was shot through with these weird vibrating balls of energy that we recognize as gods, and they're just going to do what they do. While us meat-machines fuck sloppily on this molten dirtball and find farts funny and Twinkies good.

But: why an orange? Why not some slimy intergalactic goo or laser beam to the skull?

The priestess's demeanor changed. As if the orange was a live bomb. She swallowed hard and set down the orange gently.

Then the orange rang like a telephone.

"Oh no. I can't," she said. "Not yet. I'm not ready. I'm not prepared."

"What the hell are you talking about?" Tone-Bone asked. "What the fuck is going on?"

The birds in the cages went apeshit. No one could think straight.

"Quit it. Stop that ringing. Jesusfuck."

The priestess was paralyzed. She didn't dare touch the ringing orange. It vibrated like a broken planet on the table.

Tone-Bone yanked the knife from her boot and cut the fruit in half to make it stop. It split evenly. Two halves falling away. The priestess gasped. Tone-Bone felt the bottom of her guts tug downward.

And there, inside the orange, was nothing. Just blackness. Pure infinite black. Like the hiddenness inside the space between stars.

"That's not an orange," Tone-Bone said.

"I think that's the point."

"I'm not eating it."

For both of these women, there was a cellular urge to press a fingertip into the darkness. Just to see what happened. What it would feel like. And for both, the risk was acceptable. Like, if the finger came off, so be it. Just a finger, right? (Tone-Bone idly thought of cutting the Nazi's thumbs off…How satisfying it was…how it'd feel to *give* or *donate* or *sacrifice* her thumb to the orangey black hole and—) The orange did not give her that feeling of attention and necropotence. That was absent here. This was something else.

The priestess knew the orange was gaping and enticing, but this wasn't the time. Portals like this weren't meant to be abused. They should be kept guarded, studied. So she carefully brought the two halves of the orange together. And by instinct alone, she gently rubbed the incision where Tone-Bone sliced it. She closed the two halves of the orange and healed it, like reversing movie footage.

As she did this, they both felt like the trailer was closing in on them. The walls pulled in like they were made of rubber. Or more like the walls were cheeks sucking into a mouth. But it was just a feeling. When the orange was whole again, the priestess set it on a tea saucer and put it on the counter by the sink.

"Um, seems like that should go somewhere safer," Tone-Bone said.

"No one will mess with it. Trust me."

"Hmm."

Then the priestess drank window cleaner and snorted rat poison. Or that's what it seemed like to Tone-Bone. That's what started the revelry that night. The priestess was relieved, loosened. She'd done what she needed, apparently. This Paducah ghoul had been down here by the river throwing out all kinds of wicked signals to the stars and guess what? It worked. Well, according to her, it worked. Tone-Bone had, yes, seen an immense amount of odd shit in her days—like the last few, for example—but she still kept a strong aversion to fantasy. Once a skeptic…

But the orange changed her. Fruit shouldn't yawn existentially. And plants don't grow from nothing in total darkness.

Nighttime rolled up. Freaks showed. Like river rat swill. The dregs of society lapped up to the priestess's trailer like a forgotten ocean of plague sores. Weirdos with tooth piercings and precision cuts along the arms and droopy body parts that looked amputated and cauterized back on. They all did homemade drugs. Someone carried a mortar and pestle. They did the kind of drugs, they claimed, that allowed you to walk through trees or float above houses. They could abort a pregnancy with a glare. It was all batty shit. Tone-Bone snorted some coke, smoked weed, and drank whiskey. A clutch of weirdos cornered her and talked about the rural witches they conferred with to get high and learn about the aliens in space. She nodded and chewed ice cubes. The Fuck Offs loved it. Braincase practically had her hand down the priestess's skirt. Tasker was trying all the Ball jars of liquid. Poxy and Thorn were playing a version of darts except they were using a switchblade. And Nonsense may've already been so high she couldn't walk. Her head was plastered to the back wall and she was drooling onto the floor.

Tone-Bone popped out for a cig and just kept walking. She ended up downtown and in front of a theatre. It was playing something called *Blade Runner*. Title sounded killer. She snuck in. Lots of folks in the theatre were on drugs. Someone behind her handed her a tab of acid. She took it without looking. Halfway through the film, she convinced herself she was a replicant. A skin-job. As the credits rolled, Tone-Bone fled to the bathroom and locked herself into a stall. She took the Bowie knife and slid the tip down the transverse side of her index finger. She cut to the bone before she passed out. It was enough to convince herself.

She wrapped the finger in a beehive of toilet paper. And she left the blood everywhere. She'd end up wrapping duct tape around the finger, so she could ride the bike.

The next twelve hours were iffy.

For starters, Braincase kidnapped the priestess. But she announced it first.

A few minutes before Tone-Bone returned to the inflating and contracting trailer. That's what it looked like to her. The priestess's place was breathing deeply. And she could hear the aluminum shell creak with each inhalation.

The party was total depraved madness. An orgy in each room. Some scabby puke was giving everything his erection had to a moldy loaf of bread. Various states of oral sex were amping up or decaying in the kitchen, the hallway, and the fridge. All the food had been eaten or removed. But stepping over the moaning limbs into the back bedroom, Tone-Bone found a standoff. The Fuck Offs and the priestess on one side. And those rural hilljack worshippers on the other.

Guns drawn. Faces tight. Drugs flush.

The priestess was ambivalent but trying to resist Braincase's headlock on her. Pistol pointed at the crown of her head.

Tone-Bone wondered how potent that acid she took was. Could've been a dunk tank plunge into a chromatic breach of reality. Or it could fall kaput like a wet fart. The priestess's skin was shiny like polished cutlery. And a glorious light seemed aimed on her no matter where she moved.

"What's going on?"

"Tone-Bone, take her. Get gone. We'll follow."

"Why are we taking her with us?"

The priestess loosened away and spat in Braincase's face. She moved to Tone-Bone and stood next to her. "It's fine. Would rather ride with you anyway."

Her worshippers were defeated to hear this. They gripped their guns tighter. The faces appearing more skeletal.

That's when the metallic aching began. Tone-Bone heard it under her. All around her. No one else reacted. Which made her think it was the acid…but then, it was so fucking loud. *It had to be real.* The priestess pulled her back through the trailer to the exit. Not much of a kidnapping if the victim is willing. They stopped by the kitchen sink. A couple were ramming into each other on the counter. A cacophony of angry ecstasy. Tone-Bone couldn't make out what they were, what their parts were. If they were human. Just jointed limbs penetrating and gyrating in a rhythmic fashion. The priestess poured something over Tone-Bone's finger. It hurt like fuck and she screamed, but then it was okay.

The metal wailing turned up to eleven now. Tone-Bone panicked and pushed the priestess out. The air thickened like roux. Everything smelled like fried sweat and steamed crotch. Hot arterial spray and simmering spinal fluid. Yelling flowed from the back of the trailer. A few gunshots popped.

The priestess got on the Honda. Tone-Bone turned it over. No blood. That was a good sign.

The trailer still exhaled and creaked and groaned. Like a massive pop can in the hands of a bored teenager. She wondered if this was the work of the star god with an orange, or if this was drugs. Or something else. The priestess was unbothered that her house was crumpling. Tone-Bone worried for the Fuck Offs, then remembered—no. She didn't care. They were probably replicants, too.

She throttled it. They were off. More gunshots. Panicked firing. The sound of surprised pain and terror.

At the end of the lane, before the turn, she looked back. The other six Fuck Offs were on their bikes now, following.

But behind them, the priestess's trailer had shrunk in on itself like a compacting box of foil. And there was a grasping hand stuck between the door. Someone, something, trying to get out. The sides compacted and they all met in the center, and the grasping hand was lopped off. It fell to the ground. No one paid any mind. The other women passed Tone and the priestess, whooping and hollering. Engines roaring. The trailer was now a large tight ball of scrunched metal. A stray dog trotted by the hand and picked it up with its teeth.

Tone-Bone didn't know if it was the acid or reality.

She didn't know if it mattered either way.

FANGS MEAN NOTHING WITHOUT CARHENGE, BABY

They roamed down to Memphis for a week and then back up through rural Illinois ducking out into their usual dens shared by likeminded outcasts. All told, they were gone a month. By then, Tone-Bone knew she had to quit the Fuck Offs. She didn't want to. But the priestess was now an object of worship for Braincase. Moreover, the gang fed that girl endless drugs. The priestess veered wildly between amped and comatose states every day. Still, the abductee gave them homework. And everyone did it.

Then Poxy grew fangs. Everyone took it in stride. Except Tone.

First week back in Indiana, Tone-Bone and Poxy fell sweaty into bed together—as sometimes often happened between them—and Poxy seemed sort of normal. But one day when she woke up, she was transformed. She had fangs. Her eyes were dark and intense. Totally black from corner to corner. She loved it. She started licking people's hands and cheeks and trying to suck tears from their eyes.

Needless to say, Tone-Bone stopped sleeping with her. Poxy was much younger, and something about that irritated her aging sensibilities. Other times not. Tone-Bone often tried not to fall into that clichéd genetically pre-programmed mode of open complaint about being over fifty years old. She figured—or knew—she was held together with a form of chemical Scotch tape: NSAIDs, pain killers, booze, opioids, leather, anger, a raspy anti-humanism masked as individualism. She wondered how long she could roll before punching someone out would explode a knuckle or shatter her wrist? Menopause had pulled through her life like an irradiated tugboat. Slow-moving, impossible to get around, and detrimental to her everyday health. But she'd sustained that, too. Survived, really.

So with that added to this new boosterism for all things galactic and serious, Tone-Bone figured she was done with the gang. They'd done some cool shit in the past; they'd done a lot to promote unraveling society from its made-up bonds, to disfiguring and destabilizing the family unit, to giving outsiders, freaks, and weirdos the room to continue their game. Maybe it was the undead Nazi visions she was having? Or maybe the nightly chanting that came from the priestess's room with harmonizing voices of Braincase, Nonsense, and lots of other newer strangers filing through? Tone-Bone felt the chaotic drive of the gang's original purpose seep out like a nosebleed.

The priestess immediately threw everyone into certain roles studying the transit of planets, the brightness of certain stars, and (less galactically) the patterns of ant traffic. And all for what? No one knew. The priestess took over whole walls of the Fuck Offs main house. She filled them with tiny chicken scratch. Mostly full-blown astrological charts of each member. When Tone-Bone actually read them, none of the constellation's names were recognizable. She asked Thorn, who said that these weren't our astrological signs or charts. They're the signs and charts of a whole other creature-being somewhere way the fuck away where our stars aren't even visible to them. Why then were there different signs if it was one creature? Thorn said that some creatures don't get born one time.

The Fuck Offs often hit up the Toothaker Estate and scared the piss out of the rival motorcycle clubs with their occult practices. The bearded biker guys didn't truck with a priestess who could swallow whole knives or drink gasoline for fun.

The priestess kept doing more outrageous combinations of drugs to "get closer" to the entity out in space or wherever it was. Of course, it had no name. How could it? What would one name it? Todd? Orla? Larry? Delores? Biff?

Biff the Star God, please come down to Earth and ruinate this most deleterious species, pretty pretty please?

No. Didn't work like that. Whatever they referred to this entity as, Tone-Bone often heard it as a low moan. Like a cat was in heat somewhere in the walls of the house.

Everything shook.

Everything ached.

Eventually, the priestess OD'd.

But a few nights before this, Tone-Bone was in her room, checking out how her finger was healing from that paranoid acid knife slice in the theatre. She was lucky it didn't get infected.

The priestess appeared in the doorway. It was one of the few times she looked unfucked, sober, and mostly *present* since she gave that tarot reading in the trailer. She came and sat at Tone-Bone's feet, while the latter perched at the edge of her bed. Just a mattress on the floor.

"You dislike me," the priestess said.

"No, I worry for you. We didn't need to bring you back here."

"It was for the ritual. I have no issue with that."

"Sure. You don't. But we're not making money now. We've not hosted a show, sold any drugs, or done security in months. We're fucked." Deep inside, Tone was okay with that.

"Maybe. Or maybe you'll be fucked if you don't follow what I'm trying to tell y'all."

"Call me skeptical. I don't know what it is you're telling us. People are running around like religious teenagers and it makes me feel like a babysitter."

The priestess thought deeply and was reading something intimate in the creases of her palms.

"You know. We could've been real sisters in another life. Not the false sisters these women claim to be." There was a hitch in her voice. Had the drugs worn off? Was all the endless sex and violence corroding her molecular structure?

"Another life," Tone said. "How many of those are there?"

"Maybe infinite."

"Sounds boring."

"Likely is. That's why constraint is the core of what I do. I'm holding *it* back, Tone. I hold the thing out there until I'm ready."

"Oh, you're a puppetmaster now, Tess?"

"Ha. That's what you call me?"

"You don't have a name. So yeah. People call you priestess. I shortened it."

Tess smiled.

"I like it. And, yes, in a way, I'm in control."

"Why bother? Why not let it loose right now?"

"I could do that."

"Go for it."

The priestess considered Tone-Bone.

"This is everything the Fuck Offs want," Tess said. "*To uncouple life from the living.*"

"Yeah, I'm a bit iffy on all that now. I think maybe I just wanna be far away from people for a long time." Someone in another room screamed bloody murder. Then laughter. Tone stared at the direction of the ruckus. "Poxy has fangs."

"She does."

"Why?"

The priestess shrugged. "A gift? A sign? I can't say."

Some kinda priestess she turned out to be.

"Also, I killed someone a little while back. This Nazi fuck. I buried him. Blew his house up. But I think he's still alive. I saw him crawl across the Ohio River."

"That's very possible."

"Yeah, but it shouldn't be."

The priestess laughed.

"I'm serious. What the hell?"

"Kill him again."

"What's that?"

"Kill—him—again. Simple."

Tone-Bone asked about the Paducah trailer. She watched it shrink and crumple into a foil ball and probably kill all those people. Was that real? Did she hallucinate it? The priestess said it could or could've not happened. She didn't know. She hasn't been back.

"This thing you're summoning. What if you *can't* hold it back? What if it's already here and just fucking with you?"

Seeding doubt was fun.

The priestess didn't hesitate: "Then I welcome it."

She reached inside a deep pocket of her frock and pulled out the orange. Her other hand extended for Tone-Bone's knife. Tone-Bone gave it over. The priestess re-cut the orange, slowly. But not all the way through. Not enough to split it. The fruit wiggled, as if it was an egg and a small hatchling would emerge. But no. Something dark wriggled from the slit. A thumb? Was it one of the Old Nazi's thumbs she'd cut off? The priestess didn't show surprise. She waited patiently. Tone-Bone leaned back, turning a shoulder to punch whatever emerged.

But it wasn't a thumb. No. It was some kind of bright smoke. And it *thwipped* out and searched, groping. The priestess wasn't paying attention to the bright smoke, rather to Tone-Bone's expression, which was on the verge of hysteria. She fed on that hysteria. The bright smoke whipped back and forth and finally struck at the priestess hand, in the tender skin between the fingers. It pierced the flesh and slid up and into the priestess. She sighed with erotic surprise.

Tone-Bone traced the bright smoke's path under the skin and up the arm.

"Stop!"

The priestess came to, and, in a way, squeezed the orange as if to communicate with it. The bright smoke spooled back into the pebbled fruit and the priestess once again resealed it. She left it for Tone-Bone. She set it at her feet. Then left.

Then they all awoke a few days later to find the priestess unresponsive in her bed, barely breathing. She was comatose.

Sure, it could've been the drugs. They all did plenty of them. The priestess did her share, and everyone else's. But Tone-Bone had a heavy emboweled feeling that it wasn't chemical. Her coma was fashioned from outside terrestrial knowledge.

The Fuck Offs put the priestess on an altar. Lit candles. Burned incense. Chanted strings of words. They were desperate to take a turn fucking the priestess and/or worshipping her. Braincase, who wasn't emotional, openly wept for two days. She claimed they were lost now. Broken. Divided. She started wailing and praying to this star god. "Come eat me!" she yelled. "Take us! Eat us all!"

Tone-Bone felt that, you know, maybe, um, they'd gone astray. Anything that was the Fuck Offs was now completely deteriorated. Gone.

There was no money anymore. If they weren't already, many of the women went feral. People were shitting in the hallways. Walking around with no clothes on. Openly fucking in living spaces or in the yard. It was a mess. What's worse—some women were selling their motorcycles for cash. That pained Tone-Bone most. So she threw everything she had into a few pillowcases and into her saddlebags and walked out of the house. She turned the

Honda over and Thorn put a hand on her shoulder. Poxy stood on the other side. They came from nowhere.

"Where you going, sister?" Thorn asked.

"Gotta go visit my mother. She's dying."

"You ain't got no mom," Poxy said.

"Exactly. So you can see how it's time-sensitive."

Thorn held a fistful of wires and metal and tubes and whatnot. Tone-Bone nodded at it, asked what it was.

"Bomb," Thorn said. As if it was no more dangerous than a cantaloupe.

Poxy said the Motormouths planted a bomb under their place, but Thorn defused it. Tone-Bone was pissed, almost got off the bike, but realized that she wasn't upset. Fuck the Motormouths *and* the Dragons. Fuck motorcycle clubs and gangs altogether. Thorn didn't look happy or sad about the failed bombing. She stood still. But every time Tone-Bone focused on her face, the hanging parts of the bomb moved and writhed in her peripheral vision. Played with her wrists or tried to climb up her arm. This was five seconds stretched to hours. Or so it felt.

Tone goosed the Honda in a show of departure. Also, because everyone despised her bike. Thorn slammed the defused bomb into Tone-Bone's chest. That hurt.

"Take this. You may need it."

"For what? I don't know anything about bombs."

"You'll learn," Poxy said. "You were always the smartest." A hint of sadness there? Maybe a blip of desperation? Then: "Bye."

"I'll be back."

"No, you won't."

Her sisters, of sorts. But not in the way that Tess had suggested the two of them were. How, though, could a group of anti-society anarchists and cynics form any bonds? They were sisters? Not now. Now they were unblooded and slow like a cross between a newly turned vampire and a zombie. Except they were neither. Tone-Bone only knew she wanted to get away from the house and the Fuck Offs. Which had never occurred to her—ever. Which meant something bad wrong was going on.

Something was waking up. Like that feeling right before a fight starts in a big wad of people at a punk show. Or how a riot forms. She could always sense that animal urgency dialing up about to burst. This wasn't people, though. Or animal. This felt like a long-dormant disease activating and taking over the body. She didn't know the medicine or if there was a cure, but she'd isolate herself from it. She sped away from the house, throwing grit and a dust cloud all around. But Poxy and Thorn were already gone. The bomb was in her saddlebag.

The last thing Tone-Bone saw of the Fuck Offs was this: a human slurry of women was lifting up a car from the front bumper and tipping it into a deep ditch so it would stand upright. A Datsun truck that Tone-Bone had stolen years ago. There was a whole structure back there now. It was like a carhenge going up.

That was the end somehow.

She thought of the orange in the other saddlebag. Just a fruit, she thought.

just a fruit justa fruitjust afruit justafruit just a fruitplease please pleaseplease

BLACK EGG

She motored up to Bloomington because there was a good pancake house there. That's it. Nothing strategic. She navigated by gut instinct. Then she found a tattoo parlor tucked away from the college town fare. Maybe it was a little too crowded with college kids, but she decided to cover her Fuck Offs tat with something else. A laughing hyena or a dog humping a banana. She also took the patch off her jacket. Which felt like sacrilege somehow, despite her absolute lack of metaphysical beliefs. A pasty purpled hand giving a middle finger with "Fuck Offs" across the middle. She'd get a lot less glares out in public now. That was a bummer.

She went to a Goodwill and bought a whole new set of clothes. The old ones she stuffed into a plastic bag. She rented a locker at the Greyhound station and shoved the stuff in. The yellow key went into her pocket. She'd pick it all up on the way back through here—whenever that might be. Same for the bomb. It went into the locker.

But the orange…that she kept in the saddlebag. She could always toss it, right? Just pitch it into a drainage ditch. No big.

She hit the road. Went northeast. Stopped in Columbus, Ohio for a room at the old YMCA. Then passed through the hills of Pittsburgh. Stayed with an old biker friend close to where the Allegheny and Monongahela rivers met. Tone-Bone kept on, trying pancakes at every diner, and thinking about the orange, the carhenge, the priestess. Was she awake now? Dead yet? What were the Fuck Offs doing? What would she herself do?

More importantly: what was it inside of her that she felt was stirring, waking? Maybe it was old age. But fuck age. She was as young as she wanted in her head. And in her head she was 22 years old. She drove up into Vermont and found another small college town. They were ideal. Mostly open-minded people who didn't ask a bunch of (the wrong) questions. There she met and struck up conversation with a guy at a food co-op about legumes. (Something told her she needed more iron in her blood.) Prentiss was the man's name. And recognizing her grit, offered her moderate work at his farm and orchard. He was an old hippie type. And a widow of fifteen years. Tone hated hippies, but she said yes. He said he felt moved to take her on. A little voice he trusts told him to. "I like to think it's my wife. But who knows." Prentiss was in his late-40s, always wore a well-thumbed Red Sox cap, had callused hands, drank cider at every meal. He taught her how to build a still and make moonshine. She taught him how to repair his old motorcycle. He tried to make a move on her. She almost broke his arm. Old habits.

An understanding détente ensued.

Prentiss had worked in a dairy as a teenager. His father was a high school English teacher and his mother was a bassoon player in the local symphony. She taught private woodwind lessons. He never bothered to play music. He preferred the land. Every night Prentiss coaxed Tone-Bone to sit with him and have dinner. And she relented. Then she started to help cook. Nothing fancy. Bean salad, cornbread, Israeli couscous with feta and kalamata olives. She was living, as the popular mass called it, "a normal life." She had only been on the bike once or twice, and just to go to the co-op. Some creeping mold was working its way up her, yet there was no way to discern from where it crept. Though at each moment she felt she was about to bolt, Prentiss folded her warmly back into the rhythms of the farm. It lulled her.

She was at the orchard a few months when Prentiss asked her about the orange.

She'd almost forgotten about it, buried in the bottom of the saddlebag.

"Don't go fuckin' with my bike."

"I wasn't. You asked me to get a sweater for you. It was right there on top."

"Don't touch it."

"I didn't. But we got oranges here, you know."

"It's not an orange, not really."

"Looks like one."

She stared him down to see what his endgame was. He had none. He was a hollow tube. A pleasant fallen log in a forest waiting for a family of frogs to hop inside and live. Prentiss was a foraging hippie waiting for God to bless him with a good harvest.

"Probably all dried out by now, anyway."

"Nah, fresh as steaming horse shit that one."

She was in disbelief. "Really? I've had it for two months."

"Hmm. Strong variety then, I don't know. Say, you know there's not much more work to do here. I can't keep you on past the next month. But if you want more work, I gotta friend up in Quebec who could use you on a pig farm. You'd have to work under the table there, too."

She'd think about it. For now, she was wondering how to get a rid of the orange.

Later that night into early morning, Tone woke up. Her tongue felt like stack of paper. She went to the bathroom to suck water from the tap when she heard the barn door clap. Like someone was going about daywork outside in the total punishing darkness of rural Vermont. She went outside. The barn was dark. The door open. Someone was talking up in the hayloft. She went it and wondered if this was where she should be, standing there in a pair of sweatpants with no business out here. But she went to the ladder that led up and climbed. Prentiss was on one knee under a bare light bulb talking to a radio. She couldn't tell what he was saying. She was halfway out of the trap door when she asked what he was doing. He turned to face her, but his expression was one of a sleepwalker. It took him a minute to rouse and when he did she asked again what he was doing up there and why was he talking to a radio.

"Maybe my wife? I don't know."

He was embarrassed. She let him be, not wanting to intervene in his grief.

But she did help him back to the house before she drank a glass of water and went back to bed.

A few days later at breakfast, Prentiss was worn out. He'd not slept well. Face hung over cold coffee. Cheeks wan and fingers thin and spindly. She asked after him—which was unusual, considering she could've cared less about people, but something was growing in her. Was this a distant sense of care? She'd snip it off at the root. This level of care was because of sheer proximity. She'd leave soon and not give a damn.

"I'm fine," he said, not looking it. "Just some restless dreams last night."

His eyes were empurpled with rings and his hands were those of a resurrected corpse.

The next day Prentiss had a crust of black around his nails. And a shabby collar of grime all over. He didn't eat, didn't speak. Tone-Bone worked. He slept.

That weekend, Prentiss asked her to go into town to the co-op, pick up some things. She took her bike. When she was finished, she opened the saddlebag and, curious, checked for the orange. It was missing. Her body fell into a hot flash and then a cold burn. She didn't want the orange, but she also couldn't let it go. She tore everything out. Looked like a madwoman there in the front of the co-op. People gawking, pointing. Her shit was all over, food, clothes, toiletries. Drugs in plastic baggies.

The bright smoke that she thought was inside the orange wasn't hers, wasn't the priestess's, but it was someone's. And that someone didn't want it anywhere other than with her. She was a safekeeper. This she knew. The fact slept under her nails, her scalp, her bowels, her crotch. Everywhere.

She raced back to the orchard and killed the bike. It was a cloudy day, overcast, dark at noon kinda weather. The bluebirds that usually lit on the fence were absent. The curtains in the house were drawn. The earth felt dead. The house a husk. The sky a vault.

Tone-Bone approached the front door slowly, quietly. As if she'd wake something inside or underground. It was a stupid feeling. But it also felt *true*.

There was keening. Like a petulant child sulking in a corner.

She didn't have to go far. Prentiss was in the dining room, on his knees. Again. The orange was five feet in front of him. He was bowed down toward it. All the furniture and objects in the room had been blown against the walls, smashed, broken, ruined. Plastered to the walls and ceiling like detritus after a flood.

Prentiss whined in pain or fear. Hard to tell which.

"*Help*," he said. Or managed to say.

"What the fuck is going on?"

The wooden floor slats ached by Prentiss. She wouldn't get an answer, seeing as his head was creating the sound, pressing harder into the floor.

She wanted to take the orange. But as she stepped closer, Prentiss screamed. At the same time, the orange peeled itself. As if an invisible nail pulled back the pith like a scab. Though it was coming off slowly in one strip. Prentiss bled onto the floor. Tone-Bone couldn't see where it was coming from. She didn't know how to stop it. She also knew she could not touch him.

What was going on was another story.

But she saw his fingers moving. Or the skin on them was moving. It was splitting, curling back like paper burning in an ashtray. Warping and bending every which way. Prentiss yowled like a jungle cat in heat. Blood flowed. It sprayed. In mirror-like fashion, the orange also peeled back, revealing that desperate hungry absolute nothingness inside that she'd seen back in the priestess's trailer. Prentiss's blood seeped across the boards toward the orange. Blood traveled one way. His body's skin another. By the time the first trickle of blood reached the orange, Prentiss's arm skin was sleeved back to his elbows, as if wearing a casual flesh sweater.

He'd quit crying. Maybe from the pain.

Tone-Bone smelled meat. The deli counter in a supermarket. Except it was hot. The fragrant stink of body fluids and moist holes and exposed insides. She fell next to Prentiss and puked onto the floor.

She heard, distinctly, a noise in the distance. Like a small drum being struck. A noise which had always been with her, really, but she was just now getting around to paying attention to ii. That necropotent thrum paying attention to her.

"Prentiss," she said. She reached out and touched his shin. He was too warm. She squeezed him. Her hand went through his skin. Black ooze dripping from the puncture hole she'd made. *No no no no.*

Her stomach cramped so hard, she couldn't stand. She wondered if she was next. What it would feel like to have her skin flayed off of her like a piece of fried chicken in the hands of a child.

Very slowly, Prentiss made a sound of pain, but Tone-Bone, who didn't easily give in, felt sorry for him, then she realized it wasn't a willful sound on his part—just his lungs expelling any last air in them. Since he was turning into a blackened husk. The skin withered. Papered. The hair wilted and the clothes mouldered on the body. Tone-Bone crawled backward. The orange was half-peeled and done sucking up the blood and vomit.

Maybe that's all it wanted. A sacrifice to keep going. Tone-Bone was the muscle. The orange the driver.

Within a few seconds, Prentiss's body had shrunk into an egg shape. All of him pulled and smashed into a two-foot-tall black egg striated with bulging and plump veins. Tone-Bone screamed but then choked it back.

The black egg shook and rattled.

She feared what would break from it.

But instead of hatching, it began to melt. From the tip of the egg down. And it melted into the same absolute black sludge, the darkness that was in the orange. The substance didn't flow toward the orange, which had no healed itself. No.

It was flowing toward her. She pushed herself up and stumbled. The sludge moved as far as she moved. If she jumped back a foot, it leapt a foot. She cursed at it. Told it to fuck off. She plead with it. Made promises.

To sludge and an orange, she did this.

Eventually, she screwed up enough courage to just book it to the bike.

She fled straight back toward Indiana. On the way, she spent nights awake and paranoid in motels and campsites, jumping at every sound, every creeping thing on the ground. Shadows. Wet paint. Tarry skid marks on the highway made from semi-trailers gave her nervous tics. Used coffee grounds made her palms sweat.

Finally, she crossed into Indiana but didn't feel safer. However, she felt as if the distance put between her and Vermont, between her and that demented farmhouse and that black egg soup, the better. Although, what was distance to a thing like that, whatever it was? Tone-Bone knew she wasn't dealing with acid flashbacks or botched drug trips. She wasn't crazy. Somehow the priestess was right. She'd called up something from faraway. And now it was here. Among them. Familiar with her, with Tone-Bone. Maybe even trusted her. She didn't know what to do with that.

She pulled into a motel parking lot and got a room. Maybe the first time she'd paid for one. She unlocked the door and immediately showered. Then she sat on the edge of the bed naked until she dried. She got dressed and decided to smoke a joint before bed. The drugs were in the saddlebag. When she went to the bike, and flipped open the leather flap, she stuck her hand in and dug around for the baggie. Her finger scraped something rough, pebbled. Round. The size of a fist.

Tone-Bone closed her eyes and pulled it out.

The orange was back in the bottom of her saddlebag.

HOT BREATH LETTER

Now it was a fact of life—the orange stayed with her. She did not get rid of it. This was not buddy-buddy stuff. Hold hands or take long walks in the supermarket stuff. She did not bother it. Did not let anyone else know it even fucking existed. Just kept that damned thing in the saddlebag tucked under a grease-stained bandana and a rubber poncho.

So, um, you know, what does a biker do without her gang? The Fuck Offs were dead to her and she to them. Had to be a way to integrate into life again, right? Though, what did "life" mean to her after half a century of gnawing away on time that had as much love in it as a dog's chew toy. Well, it meant digging deep into a very isolated place. Whether in a house somewhere on a dead street. Or in a tent in a forest. Whatever. Something was changing in her. No—not the orange or whatever star god's stellar spunk or blood or soul or crap inside of it. She herself was changing. Her attitude. Her demeanor. Her whole fucking outlook on shit.

Goddamn age, man. Fucking progression of time and all that. Or. Hmm.

That total psychoshow back in Vermont? The peeling of a human like a wet banana. The impossible made concrete in her palm in her eyes in her nose. The melting of flesh like a cheap candle. Shit like that could fuck your headmeat at a perpendicular angle. No no no.

Maybe that did it. Maybe *that* changed her.

When Tone-Bone rolled back into town, she needed a grounding point. A place to reassess her mental map.

Tone-Bone had one single thread connecting her to quotidian life: a P.O. Box. Nothing landed in there except outdated bills she never planned to pay from the odd one-off doctor's visit. Or a notification about rising long distance telephone rates. Mail was regular. Snow, wind, rain, tornado, apocalypse. Go to the mail. Get the mail. It was a normal-ass thing to do. She checked the box every three months, anyway (when possible). She was in month four without checking. One wouldn't think much could happen in 120 days, but *yeeeaaa*h. Sure enuff, it did.

When she pulled the Honda to the curb, it was dead noon. Sun piercing right above. Sky was oiled bullet blue. Nothing in the way of clouds. Paranoia was setting in. Which was depressing because Tone-Bone had for so long been a throw-all-fucks-into-the-wind kinda gal. But not now. Now she was listening to shrubbery and examining stoplights. Tortuous suspicions.

A few tired old men in thick-soled tennis shoes and veterans' caps exited with rolls of stamps. Men who'd be her father's age, if he was still alive.

Her hands were sweaty. She dried them on her jeans before grabbing the door handle. The post office was a new brick building. A grand towered entrance and long wings on either side. The floor was tiled in emerald green. The main lobby was reflective and dark at the same time.

She expected to collide with a mass of folks waiting for stamps and laboring under large parcels. But no one loitered in the lobby. To the left was a waiting area for a long service counter. Behind the counter was the sorting area. Lots of moveable cloth screens and worn plastic crates to hold mail. The lighting back there was weird. Greenish and orangey. Like parking lot security lights. As if mail was a separate entity that couldn't handle direct sunlight. Vampire mail. A gentle humming flowed from that area. To the right was a sinuous series of intricately designed gold-colored P.O. Boxes. They started at the end of the counter and wrapped all the way around, dipping back into at least three separate alcoves.

She liked coming here because it was a place where people gathered but didn't speak. They waited. And it held a dry, papery smell. But, again, empty. A heavy sick feeling curled through the recesses of her stomach. Like she'd eaten a soiled taco or scummy juice. Who'd helped the old, hobbling men who just left?

"Hello?"

No response. In fact, it was like her voice ended one foot in front of her face. Eaten up by silence.

She didn't look a stereotypical biker anymore. Not with her purchased Goodwill get up. No excuse not to help her there. Maybe it was a lunch break? And something smelled awful further back in the alcove. Someone got a shipment of athlete's foot and manure in a yeast box.

Fucking hell, man.

Get your shit and get gone girl.

Her box was number 351. Second alcove.

Tone-Bone dug for the key. She'd slipped it into a jacket pocket when she switched clothes. Front, side, inside. *Where the eff was it.* In the front right chest pocket stuck between a piece of sweaty, folded paper. She pulled the tiny key out and aimed.

Box 351 made a sound.

Every box had a small, laminated window with the number. A keyhole. And a slit at the bottom to slide mail into. The slit was dark. But something made a sound, a rattling. A sliding. She stilled the key. Yeah. Um. Hold a sec. That fecal-fungal smell was largening in her nostrils.

Tone-Bone was bending, but now she squatted on her heels. She leaned about a foot away from the slit.

Hot breath steamed out. Like, a cloud of moisture. It smelled super-bad. Punch a child bad. She fell back onto her ass, catching her breath. She stretched her t-shirt's collar over her nose for some modicum of protection. Barely worked. Shitty fumes permeated her nose. And the crap cloud was hot, too. Her nose felt red, glowing. She stood and craned her head around the corner. The service counter was still empty. Ceiling fans spinning. "Hey! Where the hell is everybody?"

Now she was pissed.

"I'm gonna open this up. There better not fucking be anything in here."

She had no idea who—what—she was talking to.

As a quick test, she put her hand to the slit. To see if the steambreather was still active. She felt a tickle on her palm. Like a fern frond or a bird's feather. She yanked her hand back. Were some serious perverts at the USPS waiting for single women to harass through post boxes?

What crushed the priestess's trailer? What stripped Prentiss of his skin? Who/what created that orange in the closet?

She knelt again. She looked closely into the slit and tried to focus. There, in the back of the box, something opened. A lid lifted. But nothing was behind it. No postal worker. No carts or buckets full of letters. Yes, it was a lid. But not that type of lid. What looked out at her was a massive eye with a triangular iris. It blinked.

Tone-Bone pulled the Bowie knife from her boot. She stood and stuck the key in the box. She'd had enough bullshit. She was going to stab the eye. Fuck whatever the evil orange would do to her. Not every single activity in her life could be drenched in dread. Not if she had anything to say about it. But when she opened Box 351, nothing was in there.

Well, not an eyeball.

In the box was a single letter and a thin rectangular package wrapped in a used paper grocery bag. The letter had been sitting there for two months by the postmark. The package, a VHS tape by the feel and sound of it, had no marks on it. The letter was from a lawyer. Said her uncle (father's younger brother) had died and passed some land to her. She remembered that uncle. And she'd possibly been on that land before. Scrubby and sandy. Same as all the land in southwest Indiana. But she wasn't going to turn it down. The lawyer wrote that this land was unique in one respect—it had no taxes tied to it. For a small window in the beginning of the 1900s, Indiana experimented with land that allowed buyers to purchase certain lots with a hefty tax payment up front. It was expensive, but interesting. This lot fell under that description. Thus, no need to continually tell Uncle Sam where you were by sending your pennies to the IRS. Other than calling this lawyer dude, she didn't need to let anyone know where she was.

Convenient. Someone had to know that this was what she wanted. Needed. Land with no strings attached. Get outta town. No way. The Fuck Offs trying to swing her back into their orbit? Those skinhead cumstains trying to draw her out into the middle of nowhere for some kinda revenge on their slain golden calf Nazi poobah? She'd call the lawyer and work out the details.

Now the package. It was a tape, yeah. Nothing on it except a phrase scrawled in Braincase's handwriting. It just said: *the beginning.*

Ooookay. Like she had a VCR to watch it on anyway. There was a RadioShack downtown, a few blocks from the post office.

Just to be sure, she shoved her hand with the knife deep into the post box. It burst out the backside. Tone-Bone swung the blade around.

"Hey! Hey!" came an older man's voice. "The hell are you doing? That's a federal offense!"

She pulled her arm out and saw a clump of drained postal workers washed out in the orange glow of the work area. They were shocked, disgusted. She peered in.

"Sorry, folks. Wrong assholes. Looking for a big eyeball."

One worker turned to another and said, "What?"

The RadioShack was moderately busy in the middle of the day. Mostly flumphy dudes in creased slacks and lightweight coats holding various electronic items, as if hefting the weight offered safety.

She wanted to tell them: *there was no fucking safety in electronics, guys.*

The VHS tape was shoved down her waistband in the back. She needed a VCR. Likely because she was an older woman, the employees ignored her for a bit. But Tone-Bone went straight to a wall display where a shelf of different Realistic brand VCRs sat under a shelf of 13-inch TVs. The whole set-up in front of her was probably worth ten grand.

This wouldn't be a private screening. And she'd operate efficiently. She pushed the tape in, and while not a nervous woman, breathed deeply.

A sales associate witnessed this and shuffled over. He had a fully-stocked pocket protector with the RadioShack logo on it. Total egghead. Holding a roll of coaxial cable and a joystick.

"Can I help you with that?"

More of a command than a question.

"Nah, I got it, Studly." She winked. "Tape goes in. Press play. Watch tape."

"Ha ha, yes, of course, miss, but—"

"Don't call me 'miss.'"

"Oh, erm, eh, 'patron'?"

"Sure."

"Do you have a Free Battery Club card?"

The static lines squiggled up the TV screen. They both watched. There was muffled noise. Someone had forgotten to take the lens cap off. *Jesus.*

"We don't often let patrons insert whatever tapes they wish into the VCRs."

"Oh? What do you often insert then?"

Tone-Bone leered at him a bit. She was four inches taller, years older. Her XP in life towered over any credibility his plastic pen shield in the front pocket may've held. The sales associate blushed, maybe even smiled?

The lens cap came off. The sound cleared.

Oh fuck.

It was that carhenge they'd built. The Datsun was the keystone. Sounded like Thorn was filming, talking. Braincase was leaping all over the place in excitement. She was covered down the front in blood like a distracted butcher. It was dusk. Probably months ago. Thorn's camera handling was wobbly, erratic. There, on the Datsun, the priestess was attached to the upended truck with ropes. Maybe she was nailed to it. Hard to tell. She was, though, disemboweled. That was clear. Nonsense and Poxy were running around, also bloody. Their own blood? Who knew? But they were carrying around glistening viscera that wasn't their own. Dogs bayed. Chemical fires burned in fifty-gallon drums. It was a fucken nightmare in a junkyard. Hopeless was chanting in a foreign (likely not earthlike) language and her body was morphed and corrupted and when she stuck her tongue out it looked like there were two of them moving around separately.

Tone-Bone literally heard the sales associate *gulp*.

Thorn zoomed in. Tone leaned in and squinted. Yes. The priestess was still breathing. Her eyes were wide open. Her mouth loose, wet. Thorn asked a muffled question, something sarcastic. She zoomed further on the priestess, who coughed wadded clots of blood, green and brown and orange. The Fuck Offs behind the camera cheered.

The sales associate was sweating. "What is this? A horror movie?"

Now everyone in the store was gathered, watching. A mother and her small son had entered looking for a RC race car and some AA batteries, but when she saw what the congregation in back was viewing, she scurried out. The boy cried.

Tone-Bone turned to this soft pillow of a soul. This sales associate. This walking cheese cube with glasses. She placed a hand on his shoulder. He stared into her eyes. Hopeful of an answer that didn't violate the RadioShack Employment Guidelines.

"No. It's a human sacrifice."

When he twigged it was real, he doubled over and turned for the waste can behind the counter. Up came the Pepsi and pimento loaf. She couldn't blame him. She possessed a cast iron constitution for blood and guts, but even this shit was cracking her. More because she wished the priestess hadn't deluded the Fuck Offs into thinking that she had answers. Whatever was in the orange or whatever they'd wanted to come to earth—it wasn't a solution, not even in Braincase's own narrow definition of self-destruction.

She fast-forwarded the tape through day, night, day, night, day, night, and so on. Still the priestess was breathing, still with no insides, and still the fires burned, the dogs bayed, the women whooped, hollered, wailed, whined, moaned, prayed, cursed. The whole gamut.

The other men who'd gathered around were backing away, whispering. So, okay, that's enough. It fried her circuits and all the gentlefolk here in RadioShack. Let's get that tape out and skedaddle, right? Tone-Bone hit the eject button. The tape popped out. But the image on the screen of the priestess suffering still continued. Sloggy. Slow and scattered. The faces were deformed. The sounds slurred.

Hmm.

At this point, what's not suspect? What's not actively trying to disarticulate her reality one boring moment at a time? She considered the acid. Maybe all of this was acid flashback. Or a bevy of whatever illicit and basement laboratory mad-scientist chemical cook-up she'd ingested through the years. Could be that. Sure. Why not? But she'd been around the sun a few times and nothing like this had ever surfaced. Moreover, every surface under her fingertips felt pebbled—like an orange skin. She was prepared to reach into her own mouth and pull her lungs out and drop them on Sales Associate's face: that's how badly she wanted her reality to leave her alone.

Some people edged closer. Another worker asked how she was doing that. Was it a trick? Was she a magician? She didn't speak. Just backed up to the door, keeping her eyes on the row of TV screens. Tone felt for the priestess. She liked Tess and didn't want her dead. That was a strange feeling. The need to want to save and not suppress or destroy. To maim. The camera was zooming in on the Tess's agonized face. It was pale and wet like the skin under a Band-Aid. But she wasn't getting fixed. The face slowly sagged and moved and then her eyes went black. Light emerged from her mouth like a solid shape.

The priestess turned to the camera.

People backed away from the TV shelf now.

From every speaker in that RadioShack—child's toy, stereo, monitor, public address—a brutish and haggard voice emerged.

Grrrooooow.

Grow.

The TVs shook. The VCRs' parts spun inside. The paper tape on the desk calculators spooled off.

Sales Associate shoved his way through the crowd with a Louisville Slugger over his head and brought it down, business end first, onto the offending television. Absolute madness. Glass, wood, plastic, wires. A fucking mess. There went a few months' worth of paychecks.

The RadioShack guy kept wailing nuts and smashing the TVs and VCRs. He heaved, drooling, under a massive ad campaign poster for Maxell cassette tapes. *Get blown away.*

"Gary!" someone yelled. "Not the TRS-80s!"

Gary wrecked the hell out of thousands of dollars' worth of computer power.

On the shelf next to Tone-Bone was a Walkie talkie/CB unit in the box. Since everyone was distracted, she slid it under her arm and strolled out to her bike. Pretending like what she saw just now was, you know, no big. Just some odd shenanigans. Nothing seething or evil or malignant. Now that she knew what was on the tape, and what had happened to the priestess, she was going to try and ground herself in a lifestyle that wouldn't require her to drink five bottles of mezcal afterward to forget it.

She was going to hide in the woods. For a long time.

She hoped interdimensional entities disliked the woods.

She wouldn't bet her life on it.

But only one way to find out.

LIVING ALONE

The small patch of land already had an old cabin on it. Something the uncle must've hammered together. Likely a place to stay while he hunted. She didn't know. It was a basic-ass shelter. But roomy. She needed to fix it up. Patch holes. Insulate. Maybe new glass panes for the windows, re-hang a door. The porch stairs needed knocking around. There was a well hook-up, which was nice. A latrine pit dug out back with an old outhouse on top. She'd get a septic tank or something. Or just shit in a hole in the ground. Buy bags of lime. Whatever.

She wanted dogs. Two of them. Maybe she'd start some fruit trees on the land out back. In honor of Prentiss—

God Prentiss what the hell was going on with the orange man what should I do with the orange? bury it? no

—and build a still. Make some jars of shine.

She made one final trip to town. She left a letter at the tattoo parlor for a "friend." The next day, someone drove down the grown-over road to her cabin in a massive red and white Ford F-150 with jacked-up wheels. She watched with binoculars from the front porch.

A massive man with a handlebar mustache got out and loped through a lot of brush and then through a wide field of wood reed grass.

"Big Tiny" Michael Keller. He'd done some of her tats. He knew about her, her life, her entanglements with the Fuck Offs and so on. Big Tiny didn't know about Tess or the orange or any of that nonsense. She knew that he lived with his father and that his mother had died some time back. It was rough going. Keller was, for some reason, a man she could stand. She had no feelings against him or for him. He just let her be.

She waved him up, and, in a surprise move, hugged him. He was surprised, too, but accepted.

"Hello, eager young space cadet," she said.

"Howdy."

"Like the digs?"

"Wiping your ass with corncobs, I bet."

"Almost there."

She wanted Keller to be her "getter." He'd get shit for her so she didn't have to go into town and get familiar or recognized.

"You got no money to pay me," he said. "I mean, I'm happy to help but I got a job—"

"Shut up. Yes, okay. I know. I'm not asking for much. Maybe once every couple of months. And I got money. I've buried more money in plastic bags in Army ammo boxes than there are trees in a forest." True story. Besides all of her prior bank deposits, she dug up a shitload of money in strategic areas and all over that part of the state. She had plenty of cash on hand to pay for food and medicine. She needed a generator, but other than that…"And I want you to see about getting me some dogs. A couple of good hounds."

Keller smiled. "I can do that."

She pulled out a wad of hundreds, handed it over. As if to say: *We square for a while?*

"That'll do 'er," he said. He shoved it in his hip pocket and smoothed his mustache. "I gotta ask, Tone. Why you wanna close yourself off? Something happen? Are you in some shit that I gotta protect myself against, too?"

"No, I don't think so. The Fuck Offs just wasn't my scene anymore. They had a problem with goals."

She explained Braincase's obsession with the priestess, the cosmos, astrology, how they wanted to uncouple life from the living. She also explained how her taste for it all was dissipating. She'd rather be alone in the woods.

There was something hesitating in her face and Big Tiny Keller saw it. He didn't know her as well as some, but better than most. He'd done a tat of Edgar Allan Poe laughing above her right breast. They bonded over that. She liked "The Raven."

"Sure there's nothing else?"

She considered telling the truth, the whole truth, nothing but the truth.

Instead, she said: "Let's say that I've seen some things that defy explanation, and I'm not interested in seeing those things anymore. I'll leave it there."

Keller whistled. "Well, if it scared Tone-Bone, it sure as shit scares me."

"Fucken A."

A week later, Big Tiny Keller brought her two good dogs. A couple of bluetick hounds. She named them Moe and Larry.

Solitude was the thing. She woke with the sun like a deranged hermit or a light-drunk pagan and listened to the insects cry and fuck in the tall grass while the hounds snuffled and grab-assed on the porch. She read the clouds and leaves. The fecund rot and swirl of it all. She plucked giant ticks off the dogs' backs and singed them with Ohio Blue Tip matches. She went frogging, something she hadn't done since she was a little girl. And she caught box turtles and admired the stark yellow markings on their back like arcane markings. The days were long, even in winter. She slept very little. And the dogs kept her warm. She kept them company. Gave them something valuable to defend. Keller would drop by with paperback books, shotgun shells, and newspapers, wherein she tried to parse what the Fuck Offs may've been doing between the lines of the local police reports. Trying to seek out that necropotence in the stars as a defense mechanism and not tuning into it and feeling good about it. Occasionally, she'd give Keller a jar of shine and a piece of a story from her former days as payment. He'd never stay longer than the length of the A-side of an album. Then he'd scoot and leave her be.

For a year, nothing weird happened. Nothing at all.

Until it did.

Weird happened.

NO THUMBS

It was purple dusk and crickets shrieking their love song across the southern Indiana wheatscape. Life had unfurled like the spiraled fiddlehead of a fern, springing open the spore into the grasslands. And the private life of a one-time occult biker with a drug problem gone mostly sober with the exception of a little homemade 'shine now and again was in full stride. The Midwestern moon offered no light so the world was blackening to a spent matchhead.

And Tone-Bone had to take a shit.

There was no love lost between her and the outhouse, but it worked. It was just her, of course, and some days she didn't even go to the shitter. Just squatted in the grass and peed. Living alone did weird things to one's bowel movements.

But this night something was tearing up her guts. Too many canned beans.

The night was warm. She had an old Led Zeppelin t-shirt on and a pair of gym shorts. She always wore a pair of Wellington boots when she hit the outhouse. She pulled those bastards on. Grabbed a Maglite and a week-old newspaper in case this took a long time.

Moe and Larry flopped their tails on the porch as she walked by.

"Don't burn the house down while I'm gone, boys."

She dropped trou and sat. The big bag of lime was next to the pot with a scoop in it. There was no lock on the door. No need for one. But it closed enough to give a sense of privacy. Mostly dark in that nightsoil closet. She tried to read with the flashlight an article about a supposed gas leak at a cemetery from a broken eternal flame. She laughed. She was a child. *Gas leak*. Heh heh. Then she was bored of reading. Nothing was happening in her bowels. She closed her eyes a moment to just sit. She clicked the Maglite off. Crickets chirping. Distant sounds of a state highway in the distance. Or maybe that was the creek not far away. Or a strong breeze through the trees.

Then a voice through a crack in the door said: "Guten Abend."

Tone-Bone clicked the light on and shined it at the door. Nothing.

She pulled her shorts up. She put her hands to the walls to steady herself and listened. There was rustling in the grass between the outhouse and the cabin. Legs moving fast.

The hounds bayed. Oh no.

Then the knocking. Rapping and knuckling all over the outhouse, as if by a platoon of fists. Shaking the wooden slats. Tone-Bone widened her stance as best she could to stabilize. She said nothing. The German immediately made her think of Meise. And, sure, of course, this is who it could've been. But—

But.

Wasn't he dead? Dead as DaVinci.

She watched him scuttling across the Ohio River like a demonic crab. She did. It was not an acid hallucination. That was the real deal.

The knocking stopped. Laughing. Mean, childish laughing.

She scooped a handful of lime in the measuring cup. She leaned back. She kicked the door open.

There stood a few feet back one of the skinheads whose ass she kicked so long ago. He looked…umm, not well. He didn't seem to have lips. And his gums were grey and his teeth black as the ticks she pulled off her dogs. He charged at her, head down. She walloped him on the head with the Maglite and the skinhead snarled. But he'd wrapped an arm around her waist and they broke through the back of the outhouse. Woodsplosion. He reared his head up. And like the peach-eating, cold-blooded rapist farm boy from her childhood, she threw another handful of whatever was available into this fucker's face. Lime burns the eyes and nasal passages. Where there's mucus or moisture, there be hellfire. So he screamed. Whether he was all human or part-human now, she didn't know. And didn't care to find out.

Quick lesson: Where there's one skinhead—there's another. They were like white-tailed deer. Pests to be dealt with.

But she swung the cone of the Maglite around and found nothing. The dogs were circling the house now, drumming the dirt wild. She sprinted to the front porch. There was a shotgun under the couch. A handgun in the desk drawer. She needed to cross about fifteen feet of living room. But at the front door threshold, she saw that dead-ass Nazi prick and the other wilted skinhead standing in the middle of her cabin's great room.

"Guten Abend," Meise said, again.

Tone-Bone was nervous.

For the first time, in a long time, she was nervous.

The second skinhead, who looked the same as the other, was waiting for orders. Like Keebler elves of the S.S.

"When you piss," she said, "does he help hold your cock on account of your no thumbs?" She wiggled hers for display.

The Old Nazi laughed. He made that weird hand gesture from way back and the skinhead charged. Tone-Bone thought, I'll step aside. She did. But the guy clocked the dodge and adjusted. She was back to wrestling again. Swinging with the Maglite at the bald head. Which seemed to work in increments. She wondered where the other one was. If he was awake yet? Or maybe she killed him? She hoped so. Her dogs were sadly too nice to rip flesh.

Meise said he'd come into contact with a number of other Nazi officers who'd been diligently working on odd projects before he came West. Hitler's interest in harnessing occult power and energy was no secret. But they had found something. A power beyond the stars that would remove life at will and only leave those above life to continue. Of course, in a vastly changed form. One that didn't recognize living as a phase of anything. He had died so many times before, no?

She was prepping to head-butt this asshole as Meise stepped forward. But he stopped when the drawer in a desk along the wall opened. On its own.

Kriiik.

She'd forgotten all about it. She'd stashed that evil fruit there in the oily bandanna and got on with not paying any attention to it. Life called and all that. Now she should've been shitting herself.

"Was ist das?" Meise moved toward the drawer and the orange—

the orange

—rolled out of the desk of its own accord and came to a complete stop on the floor.

"Are you a magician?" he said. "Fruit?"

Tone-Bone did not want these two men and that…thing to become friends. The ability of the orange to peel Prentiss and this Nazi's refusal to die did not combine into a banal handshake. Foul fuckery, indeed, was going to be served—and soonish. The Nazi knelt. The orange, hesitant, rolled toward him. Like a curious cat.

"You have tricks and then you have *tricks*, Fräulein."

The orange's pebbled skin was seamed down the middle. That hadn't been there when she last looked at it. Still, all this time and Tone-Bone had no clue what the hell would happen. She kept her trap shut. No warnings. No threats. If the orange pulled a Prentiss on *her*, so be it. That was the payment for housing hell in a cheap sideboard.

The Old Nazi curled his finger, as if to lure the fruit. The orange did not obey.

The seam widened, split. Like a pair of paunchy lips, swollen. The Old Nazi swallowed but smiled, enamored by what he saw in that gap between the orange lips. The second skinhead, too—his boiled grey face like a sick potato on life support.

"Shall we discourse, my little orange," Meise said.

"Fire when ready, grizzly," Tone said to herself.

Then the orange slurped. That was the noise. The only way to describe it with fidelity. A deep, guttural slurp. The rancid skin of both of those skinheads was sucked downward in an almost cartoonish way. Like the loosest points of the facial skin had been hooked and yanked on. The holes where the eyes should have been pulled down like the elastic band on cheap men's briefs. The

Old Nazi had it the worst. She heard him scream a word: *Das Sternenlicht!* She heard it syllable for syllable. She'd not forget it.

Everything pliable on them getting yanked into this tiny fruit's paradoxical, invisible mandibles.

One moment, the Nazi knelt, partially-human, fully *there*, with skin, clothes, expressions.

And in the next moment, there was a kneeling skeleton in a long overcoat, a long brilliantine index phalange curled as if to entice the orange. Same thing happened to the rotting skinhead. Standing skeleton in leather coat, jeans. The orange slurped up the meat. Left the bones. In an instant. Bloodless.

The skeletons clattered to the floor in the clothes. The fibrous peel and pith of the fruit extended outward in a prehensile fashion, a whitish/orangish craggy limb scraping the floorboards, searching and feeling and seeking. It snagged the clothes and bones that were left over and pulled them with great difficulty into the sideways mouth that seamed open there. With one exception—the Nazi's skull. That stayed. Almost as a gift to Tone-Bone, she felt. The way a cat will kill a rabbit and leave some entrails as a gift for the owner on the doorstep.

Tone-Bone was not moved. But she wouldn't gainsay it, either. In a sense, she was disappointed. She would've loved to have added Herr Meise to her list of People She'd Needed to Kill. Yet, "those beyond the rim of life and death" was likely never a group she'd have had success dispatching.

So: Orange – 3, Tone-Bone – 11.

Not that anyone was keeping score, of course.

She buried the first skinhead that she clubbed with the Maglite way the hell out by the treeline. The dogs didn't bother to crowd her as she dug the grave. They had good sense. She kept the Old Nazi's skull on the dining table. She ashed in it when the mood suited her. Or other times she would push a knifeblade into the eye sockets for fun. As a way to feel good about herself.

She placed the orange back into its oily bandana bed in the drawer, hoping that was what it wanted.

CADENCE WITH GELATINOUS BEDSHEET

Then it was 1986. Maybe a little less than a year after the outhouse hoedown.

One day Big Tiny Keller got a hold of her and asked some questions about the Fuck Offs, the Dragons, and the Motormouths. Facts she already knew. Facts he already knew.

"Why in a whore's mouth do you want to dig around info like that for?"

Keller said he had this co-worker, well, his boss, really, if we were being honest. But a dweeb, right? A sweet dweeb. A pantywaist. A paranoid, sweaty, but nice enough guy named Cade McCall. Anyway, Cade had this offer to do a catering gig at the Toothaker Estate and wanted to know about the place. The Toothaker Estate was a house of ill-repute long ago when the road it was on was part of the buffalo trace and then a site of a massacre.

Then the estate was built with oil money and the Toothakers were said to have tortured their children in the basements. Many years later, the biker gangs came long after it was desolate and made it a party barn of sorts, then the town ran them out and tried to make it a destination for fine seven course dinners. But no building with that kind of history can stay suppressed for long.

Keller told McCall what he knew, but really felt like he knew next to nothing other than what he'd heard from Tone-Bone, which was that some untoward shit went down way back in the proverbial day.

Tone-Bone said, 10-4. That's it. Shit did, indeed, go down. What of it?

Not much. I'll get back to you about it, he said. If needed.

Keller sounded hesitant—maybe even a tad nervous? Keller was never nervous. Keller, like her, could use barbwire for braces. What gives? He didn't explain. He just hung up.

And that was that.

But then, the next day: another communication from Keller.

"You know anyone named Mr. Dinosaur?" he asked.

"Is that a cartoon character?"

"Huh? No. Real person, I think. Well, anyway this guy was the only client at this catering gig for McCall. And McCall had me bring him a snake."

Why in the hell was Keller telling her this—

"Wait. Did this at all involve an orange?"

"Umm. What? No, no, I don't think so? No."

She checked the drawer and the bandana for the first time since Meise stopped by. Still there. Unbothered.

Relief.

"Well, I don't know," he said. "There's like, some other shit. He's doing research on your old crew. Biker gangs. I just talked with him at a library."

"Sounds like he needs to get laid, Keller."

"Don't I know it."

This smelled weird now. Keller explained that he'd been trying to help this guy. He was hoping to start his own catering business, and sort of stole this gig, but now it went all sideways. This Mr. Dinosaur guy whacked McCall out, apparently. Made McCall do weird shit like feed him with a big spoon. I don't know, Keller said. He won't give me a straight answer.

"He wants to talk with you about all the 'star stuff' you told me about that the Fuck Offs got up to. Like, in person. He's got issues, problems."

"Why would I want issues and problems, Keller? I live out here specifically to neglect issues and problems."

Silence.

Tone-Bone swallowed. There was nothing in her throat. But there was also something in her throat. A solid pellet made of invisible fear. What the hell was happening to her?

She thought of the priestess sitting at her kitchen table in her trailer down in Kentucky. Smiling. Young. Alive. Barefoot with sunken eyes and giving tarot readings.

Not anymore.

How much would it mess her up to talk about the past with some stranger? Some? A little? Maybe it would do her good to put all the parts together? Be a *nice* person for once.

Ugh.

"Fine," she said. "But you two can't stay more than a half hour, okay. In and out. And don't let him follow the directions here."

"I'll drive him. I'll switchback."

Tone-Bone was suddenly nervous. She'd never had guests.

Living ones, anyway.

True enough, this Cade McCall guy was weird. Definitely had issues. He looked stressed out, pale, split in half. As if part of his brain was boiling in a vat of acid on Mars and the other half was doing his taxes in the office. But—the dogs liked him. That was a good sign. Couldn't be all that bad.

She offered the guys moonshine in jars. They sat in the living room.

She wondered if the orange would get upset. Hearing all this intergalactic shit. Want to make an appearance. She eyed the drawer off and on.

"What do you want to know", fella?"

"Everything," McCall said. "Why did the graveyard blow up?"

She hadn't heard that one before. She said she didn't know anything about it. But then she remembered that she'd read months back that there was a gas leak, right? Maybe that was it. McCall said it wasn't. "That's what they want you to think."

He knows something and isn't telling me, she thought.

So she started in, telling about how the Fuck Offs met, did gigs, made money, did drugs, stole shit, ran fights, knifed people (when necessary), their beefs with other gangs, and so on. Then she got into kidnapping the priestess and bringing her back. She didn't mention what happen to her bike or the trailer, but she did tell him about how the remaining Fuck Offs gutted her, hung her up.

Keller's mouth hung open. His handlebar mustache drooped. "How do you know that happened?"

Tone-Bone stood and went to a drawer in an old armoire. She pulled out the tape. The one she plucked from the P.O. Box. She threw it at McCall. He read the label. "The beginning?"

"On that tape, which I've watched precisely *two* times, and you'll not get me to watch it anymore, you'll find the whole process I just described filmed and then transferred to videotape. The tape covers a week."

"A week? Why?"

"Because that's how long the priestess kept breathing after they cracked her chest open like a walnut shell."

McCall told her some crazy shit in return. How this Mr. Dinosaur guy-thing-being claimed to eat people backwards. It started with all the objects they ever owned, then their corpses. Sometimes it went the other way. Bodies first, then everything they touched. Mr. Dinosaur wanted to use Cade as some assistant to do his bidding here. Could this all be connected?

Hmm, well, smart guy, yes, yes it was, she said.

More importantly, was the orange connected to this Mr. Dinosaur, the name McCall gave it?

Again, that back-of-the-neck feeling of necropotence was wafting off McCall like visible stink lines. The orange was, if anything, maybe, anti-necropotent. Not good. Just…there. Just… *not* whatever Mr. Dinosaur the Star God was.

Tone-Bone explained that whatever this thing was that was eating everything around them—this nothing made manifest—it had kept the priestess alive as a display of power. That she was sure of. All the absolute nonsense that had happened to her in the past year or so wasn't just goofy shit and bad luck. No. Braincase and the rest of the Fuck Offs got what they wanted. They used the priestess as an antenna and dialed in some batshit entity out of space.

"You're the next priestess, then, I guess, yeah?"

McCall blanched. But also got angry, like he was appalled at the suggestion.

"No. I'm saying that I've been drawn into this thing. And I don't know how to get out or how to stop it."

"Whatever it was that those women summoned or called up or intercepted—it's not going away. It might take a break or slow down, but it ain't quitting on you."

"You know that. How?"

She pointed to her stomach. "This says so. Listen— I've got no answers, only suspicions. Who had the answers? The Fuck Offs did. And they are, I can only imagine, toast. Maybe one of the Motormouths or the Dragons has a story to tell—but good luck finding any of them. They both moved on to the west in the late 80s after the Toothaker went sour. No one's going to say anything. Maybe to me, but I'm not leaving this land, unless I'm dragged by wild hogs. I have seen my share of fuckdom out there."

As if punctuating her point, the dogs erupted into fervor. Keller dropped his shine. Smelled like sweet kerosene. McCall broke into a sweat. His hands shook.

Tone-Bone pulled a piece tucked into her waistband and stood. First thought? *Fucking Old Nazi is back yet again.* Side glance to the orange drawer—nothing doing, as she suspected. She moved to the back room to clear it and was stopped by the light. A small box of light on the far wall. She tried to find a source. But it seemed to appear from nowhere. Keller and McCall joined her. The light was a tape. Footage from *the beginning*. The Radio Shack footage. From the tape she just handed McCall. It played through. But it was projecting from nowhere.

Now, if Tone-Bone was not a betting person, she should've found it easy to say, *I just add all this weird shit up into an equation, right? And some kind of answer comes out the other end?* The Nazi crawling on the water, the priestess, the motorcycle and the blood, the trailer, Prentiss and the orange.

The three of them watched the footage. The men stared at the priestess's slow demise and the insanity of Tone's fellow bikers. Tone-Bone watched McCall's face. He was a rube. A pawn. He was getting used, pushed around. Part of him reminded her of people she met through life who'd never throw their hands out to break their own fall. Maybe she was reading him wrong. He could be stronger, more resilient than she gave him credit for. Probably was. But something about this guy—clearly dealing with the aftermath of the Fuck Offs' obsessions—clawed at her like a nagging cat for wet food. Like Prentiss.

Prod prod prod.

The room went dark. Dogs howled.

A phone rang. Tone-Bone shepherded the men into the living room. She went to the old, disconnected phone on the wall and picked it up. The ringing continued.

"Give me a break," Keller said.

Tone-Bone went to the armoire and opened the cabinets. Shifting magazines. Boxes. Baggies of weed. At the bottom under shoeboxes was an old rotary phone. *That* was ringing. It wasn't hooked up. McCall leaned in and answered it. His face drawn. Paler than Kleenex. When he hung up, after talking to god-knows-what, she said, "Take that phone. Take the video, too. I don't want that shit around anymore." The smell of infinity was on it. The scent of insanity. Unraveling. She caught McCall's eyes. She wanted the drama to soak in. Take her seriously. "Do not bring that shit to my house ever again. And I suggest you do the smart thing and run away. Get bored. Hide."

He was a human bullseye.

"Hide where?" he said.

She didn't know whether to believe Keller and McCall that the graveyard exploded. Why didn't she hear it? However it ended up for McCall, she was upset. He was a kid, really. Didn't deserve to suffer the eccentricities of her former gang. But did she feel responsible? Eh, maybe. Nothing a dram of whisky couldn't handle.

Larry and Moe sat at her feet, waiting. Tails beating the floor. They were terrified. *What do we do?*

Tone-Bone lead them to the front porch where she stared into the dark woods. Dogs nuzzled her sides. She drained the whiskey.

Moe's ear moved. His head tilted. Then Larry's. A badger in the underbrush? Likely a raccoon. No—this was further off. The dogs stood, tensed. Now she was nervy again.

But then she heard it. The low growl of motorcycle engines. Way off in the distance. Although it didn't grow louder or fall quieter. Stayed at the same level for a few minutes. Then it went away. Must be hearing things. An auditory hallucination.

Tired, she patted the dogs' heads and moved into the cabin. She came around the corner slowly, a tad tipsy, and heard a drum being stuck in the distance now. That bugged her. She turned to the table with the orange in it, placed a finger to her lips. *Shhhhh.*

But in the living room there was the solid black egg with pebbled skin like a massive rotten organ. Prentiss all over again. She wondered what it would feel like to have her skin ripped off. She tried to push that thought away.

"The hits keep coming. So you're finally turning on me, huh?"

The black egg pulsated, dripping tarry sludge onto the floor.

Odd—the egg had that attentive feeling, beaming it right at her. Why wasn't the orange awake?

The dogs caught scent and barked until blood trickled down their eyes and ears and anuses. Tone-Bone knelt and calmed them. *Tried* to calm them. Yelled at them to leave. Run. Flee. They would not. Not yet.

If this wasn't a Fuck Mountain to Escape from, then what was?

And then the black egg extended fibrous and gangly limbs from all around its body and a shape like a large, pocked casket formed and in its inanimate animation faced her (was there a face?) but she was overcome by pressure at her neck and she blacked out.

There was now an unwanted guest in her house. And her first guess would be that it was in the couch. Because that particular piece of furniture was covered in globs of fat and gouts of blood. She knew the couch would be ruined. There was no getting that kind of stain out.

The dogs must've taken off. She couldn't hear them. Couldn't sense their bodies around her. Their snuffling, paw shuffling, claws tapping. Their nervous scrabbling.

She was certain now that whatever the hell this was *wasn't* whatever the orange was. They were two separate entities. Which meant that this star god had been following her all the way to Vermont and possibly worked its way to Prentiss or convinced him to take her on. She awed at the naïveté she possessed. She wrenched herself off the floor and looked at whatever had taken over her space. Because it had to be, of course, the anti-orange? Yes? What else could it have been? The same thing that this McCall bastard was dealing with. Nowhere was safe anymore.

The stained couchbeast, the gelatinous fibers, the weird slippery smells.

"Who the hell are you."

Whatever was inside it did not breath. It waited. But there was *something* underneath that pearlescent coating. She saw no hands, no feet. She waited for it to speak. She waited for the tug of her skin to pull toward its mouth-hole. Or wherever. She waited for damnation, domination, for pain, the end.

But all she got was more waiting. Then the *klik klak* of the dogs' claws on wood. Larry and Moe! They hadn't left. Tone-Bone was terror-thrilled. Happy they'd stayed for her, but positive they would be destroyed along with her. Such were dogs. Loyal unto annihilation.

She heard them coming from the back room. Taking their sweet time, too. (*Go! Go! She thought.*) Walking in a lopsided way from the sound of it. Their rhythm was off. Drunk, almost.

The dogs entered the room on their hind legs. Side by side. Their front paws extended out in a gross display of worship. Snouts pointing up, like they were walking in unison or working on a synchronized dance. Her good boys. They waddled in on their small back paws and stopped in front of her. She reached out to touch Larry's belly but a gurgle emerged from him. A wet growl. His maw opened. A deep voice, like sounds from the bottom of a stone well came out.

"*Your priestess summoned me.*"

Larry's maw shut with a snap.

"She's not my priestess. Stop using my dogs as a public address system, please."

She wasn't used to saying *please*. Tone-Bone didn't have to be polite.

Now Moe's mouth opened. The voice that purged out from here was higher in pitch.

"*The invitation was offered and accepted. We shall begin.*"

"Begin what?"

The top of the couch sunk deeper into the mass of the body. An opening, a mouth. *I knew it!* she thought. The dogs tottled off onto the front porch and were released from their grip. They whined and circled and stared in at Tone-Bone through the door. She shooed them away. "Git, you dumbasses. Go!" They fled. The hole now went far into the gelatinous skin of the couch and deeper than it should've been considering the hole went through the couch and likely into the earth. Tone-Bone was willing to bet that hole lead to nowhere in this solar system.

The rumbling of motorcycle engines outside. The auditory hallucination she heard earlier was still there. It never really went away. It sank so low she couldn't make it out. But there it was. And it deafened her until the gang killed the engines at the bottom of her front steps.

In walked the Fuck Offs. Boot heels on wood. Squeak of leather. Metal rings and chain chiming. The *tsk tsk* of reproach and dismay from her gang. Braincase, Thorn, Poxy, Tasker, Hopeless, and Nonsense.

And then they were seven.

Braincase knelt down to take in Tone-Bone at her lowest. Grabbed her chin. She leaned in and kissed her. Braincase's lips burned. Tone-Bone tasted blood, shit, salt, tang. Nothing pleasant. The lips parted and a tongue darted into her mouth. Felt like two tongues. Or one tongue forked. Split. Likely cut down the middle with a pair of shears.

"What, are you sheriff now?" Tone asked. She spit onto the floor. Whatever it was had a brownish color.

Nonesense and Hopeless were hooked together in a reticular series of piercing rings and chains thru their arms. And they rode the same motorcycle now.

Next was Poxy. Fangs and all. She brought up Tone-Bone's palm and bit into it. Felt cold. She sucked and spit blood out. Poxy's ruddy mouth smiled. "Thanks, sweets." She wiped her mouth and then swiped the remaining blood on Tone-Bone's face.

"The fuck are you doing here. You belong to this thing?"

Braincase cleared her throat.

"*Belong*? No. *Worship*? Yes. This is all we are now. We've been places, Tone. Far places. You left too soon, bitchy. Shoulda stayed and tripped out, went on a solar vacation."

"Yeah, I saw what vacation the priestess went on," Tone said. "Asshole Disney World. It's a Small Crucifixion After All."

Nonsense snort-laughed at this. Hopeless punched her in the shoulder.

Thorn sat by Tone-Bone. Her legs crossed like a kindergartener. A habit of the former teacher she once was, probably. She smelled sweet, like a box of fresh crayons.

"Hi Tone. Here's the deal. Braincase is right. We have seen some shit. Some pretty great shit thanks to our Guest here. And you've been treated to some of that, I'm sure. That guy who came here? Yeah, we know about him. McCall? Here's the situation. A deal can be struck. Our Guest here is willing to advance its presence among us in exchange for some work on McCall's part. If we can get that done, we all get a special treat."

Tone-Bone was weary. These women in her home. Her refuge. It was too much. She felt dosed, dried. Like human beef jerky.

"A treat. What? Ice cream?"

Braincase and Thorn stood on other side of her. They hoisted her up. The oleaginous Guest enthroned before them passed a judgment. Tone-Bone felt that. Even though it didn't move. The mound of it leaking and shiny and swollen. The Fuck Offs laughed.

"We've gotten permission. We're allowed to let you visit the Homeland."

"Nah, it's okay. I just went last month," Tone-Bone said.

"Quit being a cuntstain," Poxy said.

They roughed her up into a standing position and led her to the front door.

"Hey, how long's the trip, Brain? I gotta piss first."

Blood still on her lips, Poxy whispered into her ear. "Won't be long, sweets."

Thorn opened the door to the outside, which, through the window had been dark and black and bleak. But now the horizon was clear. It was not Indiana. Not by a long shot. There were no woods. The landscape was all glittering sharp sand. Humps and dunes of it as far as she could see. Could've been ash for all she knew. The sky was either dusk or dawn or some netherlight that neither rose nor set but gloomed the space around it as far as any eye could see.. She could not tell. Empurpled sunburst and desolate blackness above with no stars. Distant hollow moons scattered above. Tone-Bone wanted to chalk it up to drugs. They stuck her with some LSD. Or some concoction the priestess used to choke down.

But she'd tripped before, of course. A lot.

This wasn't a trip.

Too many of her senses were crisp and shiny. The dullness of the wakened world smacked her in the face. The air smelled different. Like cold steel and the faint tang of acetone. Or maybe it was orange juice? The taste in her mouth was that of a lover's breast. But faraway was a whiff of putrescence. Rotten flesh, dying biota.

Braincase and Thorn carried her forward. They stepped off her porch into the sand.

Next to them a shovel had been driven into the sand. Tone-Bone had no shoes or socks on now. The sand was cold. Metallic. The sand cut and slit the bottoms of her feet. Tiny incisions all on the heel and arch from sharp metal filings. It would take forever to heal, she knew.

In the furthest distance loomed a pyramidal shape. A pyramid like those she'd seen in books or TV. Or no—like she'd read about in the pamphlets people used to leave behind in the motels she snuck into. Ramses. Cheops. Tutankhamun. But even at this distance, the pyramid would've had to have been huge. Unless wherever they were wasn't round like the earth and then she would have no sense of proportion. Braincase and Thorn gazed into the distance like sworn adherents. Supplicants to the burnished horizon.

And so the building, the pyramid—it moved.

Yes, two of the four sides of the pyramid flung up like wings in a lugubrious and exhaustive motion. The other two sides curled upward into a hood-like construct. Then the entire shape rose off the horizon with a rumbling flap—and sank into the metal sand, diving like a limpid machinic fish. A seismic wave shook the ground like apocalypse.

Braincase coughed a pseudo-laugh in her striated throat. A sound of fear pretending to be comeuppance.

A lump in the distance swelled and frilled underneath the cold reflective grains of this other-world. The pyramid sunk down and then swam in the depths. And it swam for them.

Poxy yelled at them from inside the house but the words' phonemes were layered over each other. Sounds didn't translate past the threshold. Tone-Bone turned, and the lit square of her front door blurred the Guest behind them. *The priestess delivered what we ordered. This is the payment.*

"You have to understand that this is all we wanted, Tone."

She looked at Braincase, whose eyes were red with grief or joy. At this point, they could've been interchangeable. And it was also then that Tone-Bone realized she'd never been one of them.

She wasn't a Fuck Off. Not really. She was a curmudgeon, sure. But never a nihilist. Which is why she tried to tear herself away from these murdering bitches, this slicing sand, and that torpedoing star god talisman lasering down on them.

They tugged her harder toward the sand, themselves reluctant but obedient.

They wanted annihilation the way teenagers wanted their high school to burn down.

Her feet bled. Her skin stung. The orange juice taste faded into the sugary suck of too much sweetness. That swollen wave neared. Its crest was one hundred feet tall. It rolled onward and Tone-Bone felt herself leak piss in animal response. But at the last moment the sand wave collapsed into a hole that shook the women's stance. When they recovered, a strong wind blew into the hole. Like a massive vacuum.

"Your turn," Tone-Bone yelled to Thorn.

Thorn let go of Tone's arm. Her skin tugged toward the hole. She tried to plant herself but it was no use. The skin on her forearm started to tug from her meat. All Tone could think of was *poor Prentiss poor Prentiss*. Small holes opened in her skin. Pores. Her pores were blowing open and thin wires were wriggling out. She knew better than that. Nerve endings. Her nervous system was being pulled out through gaping pores in her skin. Both Braincase and Thorn suffered the nervous suck. The wires of her body waggled like a child's bike streamers. There was a moment of objective beauty there. But the horror slid back in like a piano wire down the spinal column.

The sand didn't move. Just the bodies. This world, this place, only ate. It only devoured.

Tone-Bone looked back again in the whoosh and tumult of the hole and could see a large hand reach for them. Not a hand of support, but the wrinkled palm of tired abuse. The muzzy hand of a disciplinarian who'd seen enough of their own punishment.

And they were pulled back through the door and into her cabin and there was the treeline in the darkness and the crickets and no one's pores pulled open like a honeycomb and all the wormy nerves were back in place.

But the Guest hadn't left.

"Oh, you're still here," she said.

Tasker pointed at everything in her cabin. Then she pointed at the humped couchbeast. "Everything goes in there. You're with us now. For good."

The Guest's form had a distinct hole there now.

"Everything, huh?"

"Every. Single. Item. You know what'll happen if you don't."

Yeah, yeah, Tone had a pretty good idea of what would go on. Skull pulled through her asshole, turned inside-out like a raggedy t-shirt in the laundry.

"Something smells off in here," Poxy said.

"Get the fuck outta here," Tone said. "Go on. I got shit to do."

Her hands shook. Blood dripped onto the floorboards from her nose and ears. Same with Braincase and Thorn. Everyone was drawn, mercurial, moonpale and curdled with the milk of death. But she succeeded in kicking them out. The roar of departing bikes comforted her for a small cornflake of a moment. Though that was shattered when she faced the hulking *whatever* that simmered under the body of the couch-shape.

She felt it poetic to feed her Guest the orange. Like detonating a bomb. But the orange wasn't in the drawer. That threw her off (*maybe it will show up*), but she persisted and instead grabbed the lamp and crammed it into the hole. At first, she tried this without actually having to touch the fat-and-blood-covered surface. But that was a lost cause. She'd have to climb aboard the slippery mound. The texture underneath was alternating between soft flesh and rigid membrane. The same place would change density in a moment, so climbing this thing took all her effort. A trembling glissando of sound crept from the hole-depth, as if discordant stringed instruments were playing themselves out of hatred.

It was hard to be constantly afraid. Her resources were expended. It was all just trying to get through to the other side of the event. Do the thing. Worry later. But would she make it through here. How did she know she wasn't going to be the last thing in? The virgin sacrificed into the grotesque volcano, as it were? Well, not a virgin, but whatever.

Probably she'd survive. She had to join up with the Fuck Offs, who presumably had to have endured the same feat of strength. Hard to believe Nonsense or Hopeless carried through. They didn't own much.

She tossed it all: weights, pots, pans, her old wall calendar, guns, booze, drugs, a sleeve of crackers, and on and on. Dog food bowls, magazines, clothes, her goddamn toothbrush. Nothing made a sound. Items fell in with little pretense. She had no idea where they went. And who cared at this point.

"Are you the orange?" she asked, as she held the side table the orange had slept in.

Of course, she received nothing. No response.

"If you killed Prentiss, I want you to know—I'll get you back for that shit. That was cold. Why did you kill him?"

The fat on the Guest grew hard and waxy. A fierce jangling spit from the hole. The couch springs from inside it noodled upward and disappeared down in the selfsame hole. Then the nails in the walls flung past Tone's head. Parts of the roof collapsed into the fucked mouth of this being. She turned and ran. Her boots were on the porch. She had time to grab them. She stood shoeless, shoreless in her front yard and watched her family's cabin crush itself with a tornadic brew down into the hole. Even the outhouse was eaten, pulled like a toy in the drain of the star god. And the buried corpses of the Nazis sprouted from the dirt and were sucked inward. Nothing escaped. Except her and her motorcycle, which was left untouched. And the boots, which she held.

It was forcing her to give in. To give up. To admit no toehold in this world.

Everything associated with Antonia Boniface was gone.

In the total Midwestern block of darkness, the sky a slab of black Jell-O, the Guest called her forth internally. She obeyed. She stood near the edge of the form. A voluptuous and chthonic cough erupted from the hole. Gross and lumpy jism spewed from the hole and rolled down a sheet of mucus to her feet. It was filled with objects.

They belonged to the Guest. She belonged to the Guest. She was one of its objects for a while.

The Guest seemed to take a final in-suck of terrestrial air and then invaginate as if some massive flower. Like the priestess's trailer crushing in on itself. It ate away at itself until it vanished into nothing.

The silence she was left with was not deafening. The air itself was depressed. Nothing in the world moved for a minute.

She sorted through the jism and found a ball of absolute darkness, as if cut from the sky. The wholly negative space between stars, where the distance was so vast that no light penetrated it. She found pieces of metal that she could only see from one angle. A wedge of flame that she held in her hand and which froze in her palm. A wiggle of reflective tenebrous smoke. Slime that changed shape and seemed to know when you thought of it. This one disturbed her most.

The slime curled around her finger, slid under her nail. Bored, it inched around her wrist and arm. Then it reared up, like a baby bird eager for attention. She felt the pull on her skin again. But this time from inside. A divot appeared on her forearm. A hole opened then. More correctly, a pore widened to the size of a jacket button. The slime dragged itself into the hole and the pore squeezed shut. Tone-Bone screamed. Cellular annihilation was taking place, she knew, but there was no action to take.

Like sludge by a stagnant runoff creek.

The pore winked open, and the slime drooled out. It joined the other cursed objects, finished with whatever job it had performed inside her innards.

She felt weighted. Leaded. Cast in unsmeltable iron. A metal unattractive.

She collected these items and placed them carefully into a bag on the side of her bike. She pulled the boots on. She waited.

Then a light crunching. An animal in the underbrush? A mole? A mouse?

A forgotten object vomited by the Guest?

No. *No no no.*

A small globular ball. Pebbled skin. A beacon in the pitch.

The orange. Rolling toward Tone-Bone's feet the way her dogs would return after a long-deserved tramp in the margins of the property. It halted at her soles, waiting. As if timed.

Nonplussed, she put it in the other bag on her bike. This was her life/non-life then. Doomed to ferry objects around like a fucking delivery person for an alien pizza parlor.

She called for the dogs. There was no answer. She considered that they were sucked into the hole as well and she didn't see. But she willed herself to believe that they fled into the woods and were striding to safety, in exactly the same way she fled her father all those years ago.

She started the bike. The engine rumbled like a chorus of smokers' lungs. The resonance of the combustion soothed her. Anymore, it was her only therapy, her only vice.

She didn't know it, but the motorcycle would be her only home. Forever.

Tone-Bone breathed. She noticed something in her chest. She placed a hand over her sternum. It was a gesture that reminded her of childhood. Seeing other kids saying the Pledge of Allegiance. Scared her to see so many people enacting the same gesture.

But it didn't scare her as much as what she thought now. Or: what she now knew.

She knew that her heart had stopped. Or slowed to the beat of a deeper drum far inside the liquid nickel of the world.

AWFUL AT
A MINIMUM

Tone-Bone beat her chest with emergency medical bashes. There would be no jump-starting this.

And yet—*tuh-thump*.

There was a beat.

But then nothing again. Not for another five minutes. Maybe longer.

Tuh-thump.

Her heart had slowed to a mollusk-like pace.

She was being kept alive for some purpose.

That's what Tone-Bone was seeing in this warped illumination in her mind. She trusted these visions. They spoke directly to her. She didn't want them, but there you were. Like, who gets to turn down That Which Makes You Nothing By Its Very Existence?

No one gets to, that's who. *No one.*

Tone-Bone was just a delivery boy. On her simple delivery bike. On her way to meet other delivery gals. She would take these organs, these impossible objects, to the Toothaker, that old rotten pile. And then she'd be on her goddamn merry way, thank you very much. A woman of her age just wants to fucking relax, you know? Flying pyramids, gelatinous couches with living entities underneath, obsessive oranges—it was a bit much.

She opened the saddle bag with the objects in it and smoke rolled out. She heard a voice speaking from inside of it. Cade McCall. He asked for her.

She told him to meet her. There was to be an exchange. At the Toothaker Estate.

Again, it should be repeated that Tone-Bone had seen any number of insane events in her life. Consider the farmboy. All that cold blood. Her knuckles chilled at the thought of him. She never wanted to think of that moment. Why couldn't her memory warn her before it played back that particular part of tape? *Keep the awful at a minimum*, was her new working motto these days.

When she arrived at the Toothaker Estate, no one spoke. Not to each other. Not out loud. Nothing. It was all silent distraction and misdirected eyeglances. She knew every single one of these women had the same thing happen to them. That they were all running on one heartbeat every five minutes. Hopeless finally looked her name. Her face was pale-soaked and redolent with death. Something furry crawled out of her ear canal and into her hair. She didn't seem to notice.

Tone-Bone hadn't been back to the Toothaker in a long goddamn time. Blurry fragments of puking in the woods or pissing in the corner of an upstairs bedroom. Drugs taken, drugs snorted, crushed, licked, chewed, shot up, shoved up the ass, the vagina. Anyway they could get it. Some drugs that seemed to do nothing but make you feel as if you'd swallowed the moon. None of it was uplifting or fun. It was all destruction for self-punishment's sake.

Then McCall walked in through the servant's entrance looking every bit as charming as deep-fried dogshit. Thorn licked his face. That scared him.

It was straight-forward, the exchange.

McCall took notice of her but didn't register her presence. He was another bowling pin in the alley of her life that she would obliterate. Just as many others had been or would be. McCall left to spread the star god's seed through the world. A bound devotee.

Everything sprang from that decision to go to the driveway as a twelve-year-old, climb atop her father's motorcycle that he'd so lovingly cared for and showed her how to operate, and then ride away on it. The farmboy, the gangs, Hellmother, the random girls she'd had flings with in all these broken Midwestern map creases pretending to be towns. Her commandment was to help the necropotent star god and now she was not even the living or the unliving, she was just barely living. She had no imprint in the world—no forward momentum, except on the bike.

Tone asked Braincase if the priestess had to die. Seemed like a waste.

"She asked for it," Braincase said.

Tone snorted.

"It's true," Poxy added. "Dumb bitch begged us to do it. Said it would redeem her."

"From what?"

"From the other god she summoned."

Tone shook her head.

"There are two?"

But even though she asked it, she already knew the answer.

"Who cares?" Thorn said. "We got the one we wanted."

Tasker shot finger guns at her. "Don't be a stranger, Toney."

Nonsense, the least aggressive, waved in a girlish way and they all left.

SOME JESUS LOVERS ABOUT A FIRE

A week later, Tone-Bone stole a tent from a backyard off a quiet state highway. It was, she reasoned, an emergency. She'd been riding around with no direction for days. She wasn't necessarily tired, but there was a grinding wear in her that required rest. And for the first time in a long time, she was absolutely terrified.

I'm fleeing something that I'm not totally sure I can run away from— and my ass hurts. My wrists hurt. I drank and drugged myself through middle age but there isn't enough drugs in a Colombian druglord's compound to push this bullshit away.

The tortoise-like heartbeat was a perpetual reminder that she forever had the warped thumbprint of that entity on her. She did what she had to do. She drove on. Stopped in underpasses when it rained and truck stops to rest. She gassed up at mom and pop filling stations that had free coffee and always had an old timer sitting in an aluminum chair out front. Although the old timer wasn't much older than her. As old as her father, she thought. What if one of the old fellers *was* her father. Maybe that's why she stopped at them and said hi and appreciated the agnostic greetings they always offered, never scowling at her or the way she appeared or looked. Most of them were happy to talk motorcycles, engines, and specs.

After another few weeks, she didn't even know what state she was in. Maybe Iowa. But maybe it was some sweaty armpit in Ohio. Possibly she went over into Michigan through the night. Attention to direction didn't exist. She turned on instinct and if the road was worse, she broke toward it. Wherever she landed, that was the goal. She wanted isolation and tall forest and she got it. Some reflective green state park sign pointed her toward a camping area. Looked forgotten. Perfect. She'd take the chance. Patrolling park rangers be damned. And if they caught her? What could they do to her?

Fine her?

She stopped at a gravel apron in front of an open slot with a grill and park bench. She kicked off the bike. Her heart *thuh-thunked* for its once an hour clunk. It was now more horrible to feel her heart beating than when it wasn't. Strange how fast she got used to that. She had gotten the tent set up in moonlight and half her body inside with the burr of insects drilling away when someone spoke behind her.

"Would you like to join us?"

She backed up and stood, slowly.

It was a boy. Probably twelve years old. His skin practically glowed in the dark. Almost white hair. A ropy look to him. A sleepy, wearied smile on his smooth face. He pointed up the road. Tone-Bone spied a campfire further down the road.

"Sorry, ma'am."

"You can call me Tone. I don't go in for that ma'am business."

"Surely. Around the fire? Would you care for some hot chocolate?"

"How'd you know I was here?"

Kid pointed to the motorcycle.

Duh. Wasn't exactly a silent ride.

"Might as well," she said. She had a feeling this kid wouldn't take no for an answer. Not in an aggressive way, but in that nagging loving way some religious people excelled in. There was a love that was *too much love.* No one would screw with the bike. Everything would be on the level. Probably.

The kid introduced her to his family. There were three others. A mother, father, and older brother. Tone-Bone immediately identified with this other boy. A troublemaker type. He sat away from the fire, carving something into the top of their site's picnic table. He was dressed like a good little Christian, but he had a dark heart. Every so often he'd walk to the fire and ignite the end of a branch. He was interested in Tone-Bone but didn't want to show it. He sneaked glances at her leather jacket. Trying to read the patches, tattoos. Her hair pulled up on top. The chipped tooth. She was a sight. The family handed her a plastic cup of hot chocolate which she sipped on. They were snug in their sweaters, these people. Talking about their church and youth groups and all the good they did back home. The glory of Jesus Christ and his almighty father forever and ever amen. They always smiled. Like their souls were pinned to a corkboard somewhere behind them. Like their god demanded eternal optimism in the face of inevitable death. It didn't win Tone-Bone over, but she always wanted to ask a question to these folks.

"If you don't mind? What if all that good you're doing out there ends up not doing anything at all? Would that bother you?" All she could think of was the past few years of her life. Not that she was trying to do good. But it was the same as not trying and getting back bad anyway. It all seemed a wash in the end.

The mother and father stared at one another. Was she joking? The oldest boy heard this. Tone had the troublemaker's attention now. He laughed. He came and sat on a rock by the fire and pulled a Bic from his pocket. He would light a dried leaf on fire and then fling it into the pit. The father told him to stop. The troublemaker did nothing. Then the father said to put the lighter away. The mother asked where her son got it.

"Well," the father said. He cleared his throat. "We have to trust in the Lord that our faith will support our good works among his creation."

"Amen," the mother and young boy said in unison.

"I don't understand what that means," Tone said. The troublemaker leaned in. He lit another leaf. She realized she hadn't been part of a good bullshit session in quite a while. "What if I told you that there's something out there permeating every empty space waiting for you. That it soaks up the space between atoms but scientists are too stupid to see it there? Something so constant and old like a rerun that it just feels evil. And you don't even have to slip up. It'll just snatch you."

The woman slid her hand into her husband's. He straightened himself to make sure he was girded.

"That would be Satan, ma'am," the father said.

"Satan's an angel," the troublemaker said. "Came from god."

"That's what I've heard," Tone said.

"Still means that god's capable of making shit."

The father reared back and open-handedly slapped the son in the face. Kid almost fell off his seat by the fire. The mother quietly gasped but wasn't dramatic. More like she was holding a small breath to go underwater. The father came back to himself, as if he'd left his body for that brief moment of time.

The sound was worse than watching that VHS tape of the priestess getting gutted. Or listening to those racist jerk-offs in the woods drunkenly hurl each other around in a mosh pit. The kid was *and* wasn't in shock. He'd obviously been through this before. The youngest boy bowed his head. In prayer? Obeisance? Shame?

"Eat some fruit, Henry," the mother said. "You'll feel better."

Tone held up a finger.

"Hold that thought."

She was tired, if that was still possible, of being neutral or pseudo-good. Gross. The idea of binaries made her puke. But then so did everything else. Where was all that chaos she thrived on. She was going to end up a boring old lady if shit didn't cook soon. She got up and went to the bike. She gently pulled the orange out of a saddlebag and brought it back to the campfire. *Do your worst, you orange ball of death.*

She tossed it to Henry.

"Go ahead. Peel it. Eat it."

But the kid didn't eat. He just peeled. The parents distracted themselves about an obscure portion of the Bible. Something about child-rearing. Tone-Bone couldn't look away from the orange. She was waiting for it to explode, or grow tentacles, or make it rain blood. Something that would show these precious Christians what it meant to live in a world that didn't give a shit about you.

But there was nothing. Not a goddamn thing.

Henry tore a wide strip off the top. The world didn't implode. Tone took a breath. Now Henry was bending the rind to squeeze the oil out. He'd bent down in front of the fire and the orange oil from the peel would brightly ignite and create a shimmering and vibrantly colored flame. Bits of green. Royal blue. All in a flash. Zoom. Spark. Then Henry squirted another atomized mist of oil into the fire. His face, hand-burned and flush in the firelight, still was able to grin at this.

Then one of the flames didn't disappear. It hung there, next to the other flames.

Tone-Bone felt her mouth wet with this observation. Wet with anticipation. The opposite of what her mouth had been lately. That was nice. She noticed that the mother was kind of hot if she didn't smile so much. Cut her hair off. Make her slouch and get her some leather.

Henry didn't notice the hanging fire. It danced a second there outside of the main fire. And then it lifted, way above their heads. Tone followed it with her gaze. Then the flame sped off into the forest, toward her campsite like an illuminated hummingbird.

"Ow. God*damn* it."

Henry dropped the orange at the edge of the firepit. Near the ashes and coals. He stuck his fingers in his mouth. He sucked on them. The father didn't respond. He swallowed the rage this time. The mother leaned forward.

"Sweetie, are you okay? Don't take the Lord's name in vain."

"He's fine," the father said. "The Lord will handle it."

The younger boy recited a prayer to himself. Hands folded, head bowed. Something about protecting his brother.

Tone-Bone dismissed the disappointment about her plan. And, of course, the loss of the orange. She'd thought of it more as a hand grenade anyway. That round companion had a comfort to it, a heft, deep in the pips or something. Hard to tell. A nice amulet to carry around. Oh well.

The orange sizzled. Citrus scent bubbled from the fruit. The air smelled pleasant for a second before the acrid stink of scorched rind hit everyone's nostrils.

A worm wriggled between the fibrous segments. Red and insistent, it pushed up. But then, worms didn't have a knuckle in their bodies, right? (Also, did worms get into oranges? Wasn't that apples?) Sure, Tone-Bone hadn't actually touched a worm in years, but she was certain that they didn't have joints. But this one did. So maybe not a worm. Bending, curling, bloody. There was a nail. A fingernail. No one saw this but Tone-Bone and Henry. The parents were mooning over something the younger son was doing. Which was praying. The kid was still bowed and penitent. Maybe asleep, Tone thought. And Henry kept checking in with Tone to see if this orange business was legit. She didn't have any verifying stare to return, so she waited it out. Worked for her so far.

But then the finger-worm jolted up further and exposed four other fingers. The hand from the orange. And still the parents weren't paying attention. Henry stood up. As he should've. Tone almost did, but she got a foot ready out to the side. She had seen what this fruit could do. No need to second guess it here for politeness's sake. She checked herself for that feeling of doom. Of necropotential. All signs came back negative.

The orange rolled a bit and the hand that poked out flexed downward, pressing the orange up.

The youngest son opened his eyes, prayer apparently done, and laid eyes on this vexation.

Well.

You'd think Satan was defecating on the 'smores.

He belted a sound between a car-struck dog and the shearing of bicycle brakes. The parents were up and all questions, cooing, comforting hands. Henry was practically standing on top of the other picnic table behind them. The hand in the orange had emerged past the wrist.

Someone was coming out. Getting birthed.

Tone-Bone didn't know who. And she didn't know if she wanted to know. Though she had a feeling that fleeing wouldn't help matters. Always anchored with this orange of doom.

And her one instinct? *Escape Fuck Mountain?*

Slain.

Still, what if it was Meise again? That Old Nazi. That eternally recurring dickhead. But the finger had a feminine touch.

The youngest pointed at the monstrosity now. Henry still perched, waiting. (Tone decided she liked him.) Mother and Father gawped. Dumbfounded.

"You brought this demon," the father said. He met Tone-Bone's expression. "Are you a devil yourself?"

She scoffed. But, um, maybe?

Mother hid behind Father and he scootched forward to kick it into the fire. But the hand gripped the khaki and like that hand from *The Addams Family*, it climbed its way up the inside of his legs and over the kneecap, then outside the thigh—the whole time Father Bible trying not to curse, and failing, and swatting at it as a lumpy mutant fly. The bulbous end of the orange swung side to side. Eventually it rappelled up to right under the collar tattooing his clean camping clothes a nasty incarnadine. The hand scrunched the fabric and shook it.

Father side-eyed Tone and said, "Please! *Help!* My god, help us. You can control this, can't you?"

"I don't know. Depends."

"Please, do something," Mother plead.

Tone checked with Henry. Henry shrugged, wary.

"You go to school?" Tone asked him.

He was taken aback.

"Uh, yeah."

"High school?"

"Senior."

"You hate it."

He nodded.

A finger was inching up toward Father's lower lip. The nail on it was longer than the others. Kind of stiletto-esque. Tone wondered how sharp it could be. Knife sharp? Scalpel sharp? Flake of obsidian sharp? Could easily take the whole lip-chin complex off in a swipe.

Tone directed herself to the parents.

"Let him quit and find something to do."

"Wha?" Mother said.

"Drop out. High school. Let him go where he pleases. Job. Hitchhike. Whatever."

"How could we?" Mother said. "He can't give up."

Father tremored.

Tone shook her head. "It's not giving up when you had no intention or desire to do it in the first place. Giving your child a goal they didn't ask for isn't noble. It's misguided."

Wow. That sounded *waaay* smarter than she'd even considered it in her skull-voice.

The nail pierced the skin between lip and chin. Father shrieked. Maybe Henry didn't want this? If not, he didn't say no. He appeared nervous, scared even, but not jumping up and down for Tone-Bone to call off the Disembodied Hand Pouring from an Orange. The hand was tired of clinging or cutting, and it gained purchase by thrusting all the sharp nails into the Father's face the way a climber's crampon would clutch a sheer rocky cliff. Tone-Bone winced. The pain was so vast, the Father just made small gull noises in the back of his throat. On the other hand, the Mother crowed like a coked-up fire engine. She wouldn't stop. The youngest boy prayed some snatch of scripture over and over. The skin was starting to peel back.

Tone-Bone pointed to Henry.

"Consider yourself expelled. Now get."

Henry, reluctant, jumped down from the table and took in the tableaux. Parents, under siege. Brother, impotent with words. What was there for him here? Was this older-type woman with the greying hair all wispy and crazy on top her head and a chipped tooth and big ass boots and leather jacket really there to act as a dark savior for him? Should he question it was a better question itself. He decided not to. He'd run. And run far. And do well. Because maybe he'd stay and defend his parents he so had little in common with. Was that the right move? Tone-Bone thought not. But not everyone was like Tone. But some were. Henry held that uncageable look in his face. The look that spoke of doing more damage inside four walls than out in the open making his own boundaries and rules. Better to let those kinds of heads roam free.

But then there was the issue of Mother and Father and the Orange.

Tone-Bone grabbed the fruit with both hands and yanked back. A bloodied arm racked out like a prize from an arcade machine. An elbow greasy with birthslime.

A bet to herself—who could this be? One of the Fuck Offs? That'd be quaint. Or disturbed. Or both. Prentiss come back to life?

She propped a boot up on the rock ring around the firepit and tugged like a farmer on a foal's legs. The orange bloomed open the other end like a flower. Father's face shred into ribbons as the claws of the hand slashed down. A ribboned rainbow of blood and a penitent woman next to the husband to capture the juice.

On the dirt between Tone-Bone and the couple—the boy now entranced in some mystical presence and ignorant—lay a naked woman. Born of an orange.

Not a stranger, though. Oh no. Uh huh.

Tone squatted and grabbed the newcomer by the arm.

Tess. The Priestess of Paducah.

The one and only. Back by popular demand. A second show, wholly different from the first, folks! Or so one hoped.

The priestess, freed, faced her rescuer and grinned. Sleepy-eyed. She flung gobbets of Father flesh off her nails and into the fire. They sizzled the same as the orange did a minute before. Cosmic slime clumped all over her but especially in her armpit and pubic hair.

Tone thought: If she says, "Orange you glad to see me?" I'll take the top of her fucking head off and eat ice cream out of it.

"Hello, Antonia," the priestess said. "Miss me?" She tried to straighten herself out, wipe down wrinkled clothes, but there were none. Her nails had shrunk back to normal size and she wiped birthing sludge from her eyes and eyes. She pressed a thumb against a nostril and blew mucus into the fire. She looked like that teenager from that crazy goddamn movie, shit, what was it—*Carrie!*—where the girl was drenched with blood. Yeah, yeah. Tone saw it in the theatre. That was a screwed-up show. Not as screwed as this.

Pleasantly surprised, Tone nodded. She *was* happy to see her. She *did* miss her. In a strange and awkward way. Maybe it was age catching up. All that riding alone. Fighting for herself. Keeping herself aloof, away, separate from others that actually would do something for her as opposed to want something from her. For someone with an active aversion to making a human connection, there was a small growing clot of glee in her. She helped the Tess up and tried to cover her or shield her from the couple: an odd instinct for Tone-Bone. If anything, she wanted to face Tess. She was good-looking. Smoking, really. For a reanimated trailer park cult priestess, that is.

Henry hadn't got gone. He was in the flickering shadows, watching all this. Suddenly compelled. The priestess caught this and lured him toward her with the same finger she sliced his father with. As if under a mechanical order, he came. He didn't leer or stare. He held her gaze as a long-lost son would his mother. She took Henry's head in her hands—something Tone-Bone would not have recommended no matter how attractive this fruity dead girl was (Tone was kinda real gone, too, though?)—and valued it, from this side, then from that side. Then she leaned in and whispered into Henry's ear. A question.

"Yeah, I think so," Henry said.

"Good. Go get it and bring it here."

Henry sprinted away into the dark past the reach of the campfire. The family car had to be around in there. Tone was willing to bet her Honda that Henry hadn't run that fast in his life, ever. Father, Mother, and Prayer Boy were plopped onto a log, all of them nursing the slashed chinny-chin-chin. Tess was bouncing on her toes. Swaying her head from side to side like she was waiting for a lover to step off a Greyhound bus. The slime splattered onto the family.

She stopped and her eyes focused. Listening.

"You hear that?"

"What? Henry?"

The priestess shook her head. Uh huh. Nope.

"Something else. Too far away for you to hear."

"Why you asking me then?"

"*Shhhhh.*"

The family was scared, peering into the dark beyond, behind. Above. Even the bloodied dad.

"We need to leave," the priestess said. "Now-ish." Henry jogged back, out of breath, with a hunk of metal in his hand. A pair of pliers. "But first…" She made a sweeping motion, inviting Henry to approach his father. Barely able to hold his head up now, and Mother side-straddling him, Father raised his head expecting some kind of respite, although he should've been paying more attention in the past minute or so. Henry put a hand on his dad's forehead and stared into his eyes. He scanned the teeth and chose the upper right canine. Henry tapped it lightly with the tip of the tool. The pliers opened and gripped. The family were like patient dogs. They'd never invited a nihilistic (or once nihilistic) biker into their circle of trust before. Henry levered his arm up. The roots snapped like thread tearing in a hem—

No, Tone thought too fast to register, it was the sound of a boot crunching softly on the glass of a busted-out car window, heel to toe, *kraaack krunchchch*—

Father wailed. Then fell to moaning. The slashes in his face hurt more. Mother gasped. Blood, very little of it, dotted the youngest son's face. Henry dropped the tooth into the priestess's open hand. Tone-Bone was changing—from one time fuck-it-all mentality to something more, well, *softer*. Not that soft. Like going from adamantium to steel. That kind of soft. Yet she wasn't keen to stop Henry from violating his Father's dental record. Why? Because she sensed a hot shame from this kid. The suffering under the hand of khaki'd rage. The cold authority of a man who had no authority other than what was written in a book over a thousand years ago. Henry didn't subscribe to boundaries, much as she didn't. Like recognized like.

Tess pushed the tooth around on her palm. Then she threw it back into her mouth like an aspirin. She didn't swallow it. Instead she rolled it around her mouth as a piece of candy. Then she spit it back out onto Henry's palm. It was the brightest object Tone had seen. Pulsating white light, so clean.

"Put that in some dirt, boy. Watch after it."

She kissed him on the cheek. A blood outline of lips remained. Henry nodded and squeezed the tooth, running at full speed away into the dark as if the light from the campsite was harmful. Tess bent to pick up the orange, healed now. Tone checked out her ass. Dead or undead or whatever, still a lovely thing. The family flinched at them. Any movement was traumatic now.

The priestess held the orange like a home, which made sense. Tone-Bone wondered if she'd end up climbing back in that thing before the sun came up.

"I got something for you to do, sweetness," Tess said.

"What? Start an orchard?"

The priestess cocked her head at that. Pursed her lips. Not bad, not bad, they said.

"No, light that rind oil again. I wanna see something."

They were walking back to Tone's tent. The priestess was paying attention to the outer dark again, the shifting nocturnal noise. Acting as if someone was watching them just beyond the treeline. Tone-Bone pulled a lighter out and squeezed some still-intact rind through it. The tiny flame, blue-orange-yellow, rose up and sped through the air and into the trees.

"We go thattaway," the priestess said.

"Climb on," Tone ordered. She started the bike.

"Yes, ma'am."

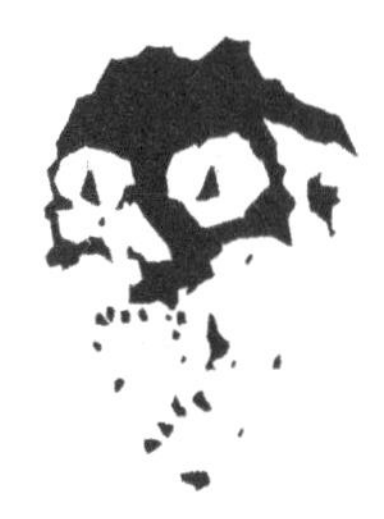

YOU HOPE
IT'S A CRINKLE

Every so often the priestess lit more orange oil and they steered after the ensuing flames. Tone couldn't imagine what it was like riding on the back of a bike naked. She didn't need to. She'd done it plenty of times. This situation reminded her anyway of taking Tess from Paducah back up to Indiana some years back.

Over the wind, the priestess said into Tone's ear: "The Fuck Offs forced me to summon something."

"I know," she yelled back.

"But someone else answered. Two separate things."

Tone cut the throttle on a dark highway and pulled onto the small strip of breakdown gravel.

"How's that, again?"

"The orange is not the other thing—"

"Mr. Dinosaur," Tone said, thinking of that catering guy. *Cade. Cade McCall.* She wondered what that poor bastard was doing at that moment. Shoving strangely weighted objects down the throats of toddlers or feeding oblivion to retirees.

"Cute name. Sure. Mr. Dinosaur. Different."

"You did it on purpose?"

"No, no. It was like calling someone from across the room at a party. Lots of noise. You don't know their name. You're just gesturing and waving them toward you. My rituals were so broad they brought two entities from across the room."

Across the universe.

"And," she continued, "That's where the orange tree in my closet came from. That was the one that got here first. The other one, the ones your friends catered to, that one came second. Or maybe it had always been around here? Listen, I know you're all doom and gloom and you've got this life you want to lead."

Tone brought Tess's hand to her chest. Let her feel, or not feel, what was and wasn't there.

"*Oh.* Hmm. Well. In any case, I'm more of a funtime gal. Not that I'll get to enjoy any of this much longer. Doesn't matter, though. I'm with the orange."

"Yeah, I can tell. The orange killed my friend. Prentiss."

Tess was shaking her head.

"Looked that way, I'm sure, but no. Black egg thing?"

"Yeah."

"That's Mr. Dinosaur."

Made sense. That's why the orange gobbled it up. To protect Tone-Bone.

"So the orange eradicates this Dinosaur fella, then?"

"Um, sure. You could say that. One's against th'other. The way positive and negative poles repel. But without assigning good or ill. Don't do that. That dog don't hunt."

Headlights coming down the road. When they caught onto the women, the car slowed, maybe to help or catcall, but when it got close enough the two dudes in the front seat gawked in a rubbernecking car crash kinda way. A bruised biker and a gore-saturated nude woman chatting? They crawled on by before picking up speed and disappearing.

Smart move.

"What about that old Nazi fucker?" The priestess made a face like *what did you say?* "That old bastard. I've killed him twice. He keeps coming back."

"Don't know anything about that. Maybe he's part of these two things or mebbe it's something else."

"A third thing from space? Fucking hell."

Tess laughed. "Every*damn*thing is from space."

Good point.

Tone-Bone wrapped the priestess in the leather jacket and a sweater for improvised shorts until she was able to stop into a Salvation Army for pants, shirt, and a jacket. She also was tasked by the priestess to buy a pack of index cards and a ballpoint pen. They found a Denny's, ate breakfast, and Tess drew up her Tarot deck on the index cards. Then she performed a reading for Tone. Among the drops of syrup and old people chortling over coffee, Tess found that they needed to eradicate something that had been haunting Tone-Bone almost her whole life.

However, Tess reported that she couldn't help Tone with any of it. "I have to stay outside of the scene, hun."

"Do I have to kill anyone?"

The priestess was sullen. Unhappy to report the affirmative on that question.

Tone didn't acknowledge that openly but knew what she meant.

It was all wishy-washy and vague to Tone. But Tess confirmed that they would keep following the flames. Turns out they would be on the road forever, then. Her initial instincts on that matter bore out.

Tess kept reading, turning over cards like The Gargling Frog and The Eight Actors. Tone stared into a cup of coffee and had a short waking dream. Maybe even a hallucination.

It was a fully realized conversation with her father that Tone remembered having with him—but she knew it wasn't real, though it *felt* real—about how he went away to the war and came back and she thought he was lucky but he said he'd go again in a minute if it meant fighting the Nazis. And she wondered about how she dodged that call in life. She did security *for* Nazis because her world was motorcycle clubs and white supremacists working on the same side of the anti-law thing. But now she knew how ludicrous that was and should've murdered them all where they stood.

"So you'd go again? Leave me," she said to her father.

He looked past her because he couldn't look at her.

"Where do I sign up," he said.

"Why?"

Now he looked at her. She hated that he'd treated her so much like a grown up. "I'd be gone so you could keep living. Here. It's easy. Yes or no. Ask me if I'd fight fascism. Go on."

"Would you?"

He nodded first because he couldn't bring himself to confirm to her face.

"Yes," he said.

Antonia, in her waking dream, cried so hard she shook herself out of her reverie and spilled coffee all over the table, soaking the homemade Tarot cards and irritating the waitress not a little bit. Tess didn't mind because she had a good idea of what was going on in her friend's head and couldn't do much to help it.

FISHBEARD'S FEAST

Tess called the shots. She suggested that they go after those who may have been or will be *seeded* by the star god, the anti-orange.

Tone was lying in a half-submerged state of consciousness among a stand of pines by some rural highway as Tess was weaving bracelets with tender plants and roots and rotting detritus. It was the only thing they could do now. Would it be hard? Yes. Impossible? Maybe. Worthwhile? Definitely.

If they didn't pursue this, their lives—whatever that word might mean for these two beings—would revolve around stopping at motels and pitching down for sleep behind those roadside tabernacles that somehow combined the business of selling porn mags and fireworks. Or Christmas decorations and steak knives. Those desolate areas of saplings and trash behind these buildings, littering the ground, were the non-spaces of America. No one wanted to look there. And no one did. In any case, motel rooms were often gotten for free by using the priestess as fleshbait for the late-night motel desk clerks who inevitably were lonely men who didn't have the mental fortitude to resist her. Or sometimes they just slipped into a motel room when the door was left unlocked. Which said doors were, and often.

Each one of the people Tone and the priestess would come to encounter had been courted and contacted by the star god. But none of them—so far—had been sent on their way to seed these impossible objects out into the world. This was based on the priestess's Tarot readings and scrying of her previously crafted implements from pine needles, twigs, and shed bird feathers.

The first lighting of the orange oil created a globular flame the color of a ruby. It moved fast. So the women rode fast. The flame led them to a small town in Oklahoma and a teenage goth named Amanda. They rolled up to a small saltbox home in a working-class neighborhood at night. Tone hadn't been loitering outside the girl's window long before she heard the mother yell her daughter's name. *Goddamn it, Amanda!* The room was papered with posters of sad-faced Dark Wave bands and occult symbols. Tone's kind of gal. Amanda was pledged to the darkness well before this Mr. Dinosaur came down for a visit. Made sense why she would seek it out or welcome it. But that was perhaps too dark, Tone-Bone thought. And then she thought: *I'm getting too gooey.* Amanda's face was naturally pale with make-up and kohled eyes. Black lipstick. Spiky black hair like a wave-tossed sea anemone in the great plains. Lots of metal in the ears. A studded necklace. She was slight but fierce.

How far was she in the seeding process? According to the priestess, Mr. Dinosaur reached out and built a connection.

"Yeah, I know all about that," Tone said.

They waited. It was dark by early evening. They stood by the bike in the street a few houses away. Amanda's bedroom light was on. Her mother—a single parent by the looks of it—had taken off an hour before.

"What's our plan here?" Tone said.

"I've considered this."

The priestess *almost* looked normal in her stolen get-up. She opened the saddlebag with the orange and took it out and held it up in the copper colored streetlights.

"We feed a wedge of this to each person we find," she said.

"Simple as that?"

"Simple as that."

"You've never tried to get someone to unwillingly eat have you?"

The priestess stared.

"It's like forcefeeding a cat," Tone said.

They didn't have a chance to feed anything, though, because Amanda got into a piece of shit Plymouth Horizon the color of pencil lead and chugged away down the street.

Amanda the goth worked nightly at a fried fish restaurant in the ragged downtown. Slippery ceramic tile floors. Grease-covered everything, all the time. The drop ceiling had water stains and sagged here and there. The tables were sticky with dried soda and the whole affair smelled fairly rancid. She worked the drive-thru window. Tone and the priestess rolled up and Amanda's voice croaked through the tinny speaker shaped like a pirate ship. Must've been a slow night. Amanda sounded defeated.

"Welcome to Fishbeard's, what can we fry you?"

"What's good?" Tone said.

Pause.

"Nothing," Amanda said.

"Sounds tasty. I'll have that."

The sound of Amanda laughing. Tone eyed the menu.

"Gimme the Fishbeard Feast," she said.

"Five dollars and ninety-five cents. Pull around."

Amanda opened the drive-thru window to collect the money from Tone-Bone but stopped mid-way. Something about these two on a bike didn't seem to click. Like they didn't belong in this reality the same as she felt that *she didn't belong*. Was that good or bad?

The priestess waved. She wore no shoes. "Hi, Amanda."

"How do you know my name?"

Tone said the priestess knew most everyone's name. "But it's on your nametag. Also, we know you're friendly with a weird voice that talks through your Walkman, yeah?

Amanda pulled back into the window a bit. Satisfied by her hunch about these two.

"Fuck you, weirdo. What are you, stalkers?"

"Hey, we're all weirdos here," Tone said. "Calm down. We just want to know what that voice has said to you?"

"Did it make promises?" the priestess said.

Another teenaged worker finished the Fishbeard's Feast order and looked over to Amanda.

"Everything cool, Mandy?"

His nametag said JAMIE. There was a gold star sticker at the end of the name.

"Jesus Christ, Jamie, I said quit calling me that. No one calls me that. Do I look like a fucking 'Mandy' to you?" She turned back to the drive-thru window. "I'm calling the cops. Buzz off." She shut the small doors on the women.

"I told you," Tone said over her shoulder.

She revved the bike. The priestess got the signal and leapt off the back. They were starting to communicate through pheromones or telepathy at this point. Tone peeled off to go around and inside the restaurant. The priestess pried opened the drive-thru window with her fingernails and pulled herself inside like a child with wiry strength.

Amanda watched in horrific reverie.

"We can't serve you if you come back here," Jamie said.

Tess righted herself and approached Jamie and ran a finger down his face. She licked the tip of her finger. "Yum," she said.

Tone-Bone drove her bike through the double front doors. The bike was deafening in the small Fishbeard's dining room. The grumbling engine bouncing off the tile floor and plastic booths. The bike almost spilled over on the greasy floor. She killed the engine and approached the counter. Her boots clopped and the sounds of the leather jacket and metal hanging from it was theatrical. She appreciated that. Maybe Amanda would, too.

"Hi, Jamie," she said. "Your shift is over. Hit the bricks, skipper."

Jamie didn't move. His chest heaved. His eyes wide like seashells. Tone snapped her fingers at him.

"Fuck off. Go home. Take some fish with you."

Jamie pressed the waxed bag of Fishbeard Feast to his chest and ran out the front door with it.

Then they were three. And while the priestess was brought back to life by the orange—whatever providence it may be arranged with—it didn't stop her bare feet from having a heck of a time gaining purchase on a tile floor. And Tone was just older. Possibly half-dead. Possibly not. But still not teenaged-Amanda-spry. The goth girl could just run out the side door of the restaurant. That would be bad. Tone-Bone sensed this.

"Yeah, you can run. But you know we'll find you. And your Walkman is in the breakroom locker. I'm gonna smash it if you leave."

Amanda's kohl ran down her face from sweat. Or tears. Black sticky tears. Her outward decoration had celebrated death and maybe welcomed it. But now she was afraid of dying as a reality more than anything she'd ever experienced in her short tenure on earth. And losing the Walkman. That took her a few months to pay for.

The priestess said: "That low voice talkin to ya. That sick growl? What's it say?"

"What do you assholes want," Amanda said. "Take the money and go. I'm not telling you bitches anything."

"We don't want money. We want to help," Tone said.

"Yeah right."

"We don't look it. But we do."

The outside had turned totally dark. The downtown was dead. No one was hanking for fried fish this night. The triangle of women stared each other down waiting for a move or an intercession. Out the window at a four-way, Tone watched the stoplight turn green to yellow to red.

Then the red light grew dark. Like old blood. It flashed.

Then it went blank.

Static crackled in Amanda's headset and the speakers in the ceiling that had piped in synthesized sea chanteys.

Aaaaamaaaaaanduuuuuuuh.

A couple gross drop ceiling tiles loosed and fell to the floor. The voice was deeper than a motorcycle rumbling. The cash register shook itself open. The grease fryers sloshed and sizzled. The priestess slid back to avoid getting burnt.

The voice crowned and boomed. It shook everything deeply. The stoplight swung outside in the non-wind like a plastic toy getting batted by a massive cat.

"Amanda. Do you, ahh, trust me?"

It was a voice so old it would've made trilobites feel fresh and young. A voice that comforted the solar system as it came into being. The illuminated Fishbeard's sign in the parking lot snapped off and crashed onto Amanda's Plymouth Horizon.

"Why are you doing this to me?" she yelled at the ceiling.

Tone-Bone asked Amanda what the voice had been telling her.

Amanda was scared and ashamed. Confused. All of it sounded insane. And now she knew it actually was.

"The voice played between the songs on the Cure tapes. It wanted me to help it. To give things to people. To feed them stuff in the fish or fries or whatever. I don't know, okay?"

Tone held up her hands in a protective manner. "That's fine. That's what I figured. But you know, those objects are horrible. And they'll kill all the people in the world."

"What?"

The priestess was sitting cross-legged on the orange countertop now. She was unraveling paper straw wrappers and weaving a design with them.

"That shit will destroy everything in the universe. It's out there waiting to eat all of us. If you like the Cure, then you should not listen to that voice."

Amanda looked to the priestess and Tone took a small step forward. She'd been doing this at every opportunity. Trying to pinch off her escape routes. The priestess finished whatever it was she'd been fashioning and then covered it in saliva. She prayed some silent invocation over it. Then she put the straw in her mouth and tested it. She bit the paper design and rolled it with her tongue and blew it through the straw at Amanda's face. It squelched when it hit her neck. The goth slapped at it like a bug. She swayed on her feet and pointed at the priestess.

"You psychotic bitch."

The priestess smiled. "So I've been told."

Something blew against the window and stuck there. A sheet of stray newspaper. Then it flew away. The wind was picking up outside. Swirling and cascading and churning dirt and the land based flotsam that collects in every downtown. Beer cans, cigarette butts, Stryrofoam containers, diapers. Steel trash cans tumbled down the road like giant bullet casings. The doors to Fishbeard's rattled. In the distance, Tone-Bone heard the tornado sirens. Not unusual for Oklahoma. But not the right season. Or the right weather.

"I'm thinking we've got very little time here," she said.

The priestess was already helping Amanda sit and then lay down behind the counter. Her face a dripping black mess.

"I feel woozy," Amanda said. She rubbed at her neck.

"We got something for that."

"What did you do to her?" Tone asked.

Tess placed a hand to her chest in feigned shock. "Am I a priestess? Is this a situation that calls for my divine intervention?"

"Yeah, yeah."

The priestess motioned for Tone to get the orange. Which she did from the saddlebag on the bike. The priestess felt the orange. Always treated it with respect and care. Rolled it a bit. Then she showed it to Amanda like a magician shows a volunteer a top hat or a pack of playing cards.

See? A totally normal orange.

"You like oranges, Amanda?"

"Sure. I guess." Her voice was distant and hazy. Telegraphed from another level of consciousness. "Like OJ."

"Exactly like OJ. I like that at breakfast. Don't you?"

Tone-Bone made a hurry-up motion with her hands. The wind was gale force now. Small pebbles and rocks were pinging off the building. The window glass was buckling in and out. One was spidered from a larger stone. They had to now yell at each other over the wind's noise outside. Somehow, though, Tone-Bone figured that just this city block was under duress and any stranger looking in on the restaurant wouldn't know what the hell was happening in here. Tone-Bone urged her partner to shove the orange in already.

"Don't rush me, dear. This isn't an afternoon snack."

The priestess slid her thumbnail into the orange flesh and spun it around in one smooth movement. The sections were wet and dripping and she carefully separated one and held it in her hand like a slippery jewel that was to be returned to the center of a royal crown.

"Amanda, do me a favor and open your mouth for me, honey. Time for a snack."

As the fruit was lowered, Amanda clenched her jaw.

Mr. Dinosaur's doing, of course. Telling her to keep her jaw jammed shut no matter what.

The wind buffeted the restaurant with hurricane speed. Pans were falling off tabletops in the kitchen and the employees' entrance in back was slamming open and closed. The tornado siren converged with the whine of the wind to unnerve any hearing creature alive or undead. It was like a dogwhistle for weirdos.

Then Amanda began bucking and resisting. An oleaginous goo streaming from the corners of her mouth. Amanda sucker punched the priestess in the mouth. Tess spat a tooth out but took it in stride. The priestess and Tone redoubled and pinned Amanda to the floor with hands and knees. The teen foamed and dodged the fruit at every turn like a rabid dog with hydrophobia.

"How many times have you done this?" Tone-Bone said.

The priestess glared. "Does it look like I've ever done this shit before?" She bore down on Amanda. "C'mon, sister. You gotta eat this slice."

She stabbed the orange at the mouth, and it skipped off the stiffened lip and it hit Amanda's nostril. Amanda snorted and growled. Her eyes rolled back and went red as the once-blinking stoplight.

Fishbeard's shook so hard that it felt it was about to take off into space.

The sidewalk was coming up outside. Like an old scab on a child's knee. Chunks of concrete were smashing into the windows and the roof. The only reason they weren't obliterated yet was the protection of the ordering counter and the large metal appliances surrounding them.

They were in a stone tornado.

Something small whizzed past Tone's head and it smashed into the priestess. A softball-sized piece of rock with rebar in it pierced Tess's upper chest under the collarbone and pinned her to a cabinet behind. She was a priestess, but she was also an actual being. And this being was knocked out. Tone stepped over and slapped her partner. The priestess's eyes cracked open.

"What the fuck am I supposed to do?" Tone screamed.

The priestess held another orange wedge up. Tone took it.

"And the Walkman," she said. Her eyes closed.

Tone-Bone crouch-ran back to the breakroom, dodging dust devils and pinging rocks and snagged the Walkman. She brought it back and set it on Amanda's chest. The teenager could've been going into some kind of fatal shock. Hard to tell. The foam was purling from her like water from a spring. She got down and tried to speak directly into her ear.

"Amanda, I got your Walkman. You can listen to the Cure." Nothing.

A world of shit spiraling around her. A near-comatose teen. Her partner unconscious, perhaps dying.

So it came as much of a surprise to Tone-Bone as to anyone else when she decided on how to get Amanda to eat the orange. She did something she'd only heard about and seen done but never suffered in her life. And you know what gave her the idea to do this thing? The teenager's total devotion to death and darkness and the morose. The feel bads.

Tone-Bone tickled Amanda's ribs.

She still had nerve endings. Still had involuntary responses. She just hoped that she was one of those sensitive folks.

Amanda's mouth broke open in laughter and defensive posturing to block out the invading fingers.

"Now," Tone said. She dropped the curve of orange in and shut Amanda's mouth. Clamped her nose for good measure. Amanda was forced by deep human reflex to deal with the food. She stopped laughing and chewed the orange and swallowed it. Immediately, Tone-Bone backed off. The stone tornado continued the whole time and a final chunk of concrete with rebar appendages sailed through the restaurant just above their heads. When it broke through the drive-thru window leaving a ragged hole in the wall, the tornado and wind dissipated.

There was a squeaking in the distance. Tone-Bone figured it was the stoplight swinging around. She kicked the priestess's foot. "Hey. Wake up, Merlin."

The priestess opened her eyes. She wasn't bleeding. But she wasn't well, either. She looked at the rebar in her shoulder.

"Take this out for me, will ya?"

Tone-Bone leaned in and said it was going to hurt. She yanked and the metal bar pulled out with a slimy crackle.

Amanda was awake to herself and crying quietly. She crawled over into the priestess's arms and the latter stroked her hair and rocked her. As if they'd always belonged together. She was the most maternal figure. Tone stood and realized the building was going to collapse any minute. Also that her bike was massacred. And Amanda's car was pancaked.

Tone walked the bike again because she was going to have to fix it herself.

They all made their way back to the teenager's house. No one said much. Amanda listened to the Cure on her tape player. Tess held the once-again whole orange like a healing talisman. Which is what it was for her.

And sure enough, just that little ole block of the little ole Oklahoma town was devastated. The rest of the surrounding area still looked as boring and untouched as any shithole in the U.S. of A. The anomalous destruction of the Fishbeard's in Oklahoma was deemed a gas explosion and earned little fame.

THE DEEP SLEEP

The next flame lit was triangular and pale green. It aimed in a southerly direction. Slow and steady. That was a minor relief. Took them to one of the largest military bases in the world at the time, Fort Hood near Killeen, Texas. The air hung heavy like wet laundry down there. Then the next day it was as hot as an industrial clothing dryer. It was so hot down there that at the end of the day concrete glowed with the heat. Everything near the base was about the Army. The women stayed nearby in a rundown one-story motel in Copperas Cove called The Deep Sleep. The name was unnerving to both of them but went unmentioned. The cost for one night was cheap. The person they searched for was a sergeant who lived off-base between towns. His name was Sergeant First Class Gary Bunton. SFC Bunton had started hearing Mr. Dinosaur through a ham radio set-up in his spare room. He was talking with an up-and-coming business from Togo one evening when the voice broke through.

This situation would be even more dangerous because SFC Bunton carried a sidearm. Amanda the Teen Goth was a drive-thru worker. Her greatest weapon was a stiletto insult or a wilting sneer. A soldier could put a bullet in your face. Tone-Bone and the priestess tread lightly. The priestess considered when a soldier didn't have their gun on them. Tone suggested when they're in the shower.

"Then that's when we should approach him," the priestess said.

So they staked out his small home and watched for him to spend more than five minutes in his bathroom. When it seemed time, they jimmied a garage window and climbed in. When SFC Bunton finished washing his body and opened his shower curtain, the two women were waiting for him. He didn't gasp. He didn't move. He was assessing. And he didn't seem to assess much. They told him why they were there. In the ensuing brawl, Tone-Bone got a bloody nose, the priestess chipped a tooth and broke a finger, and SFC Bunton escaped out his bathroom window and across six backyards before he climbed a water tower with no help just to get away from the crack-skinny lady and the biker gal. They were concerned he would leap from the tower if they climbed after him, but it was a risk they had to take. The whole time the water tower groaned with insidious sounds. As if it was stuffed full to the walls with an ancient and massive creature that held Tone-Bone accountable for its enclosure. There was nothing like Oklahoma. No stone tornado. Yet another relief. After they got the orange into him, he also cried in the priestess's arms, naked and shivering, saying something about his plans to seed the entire III Armored Corps.

The third flame was a nearly clear flame tinged with a light blue. It rippled and threatened to go out. It led to a mother of three in Connecticut—who punched a hole in a concrete wall when the priestess offered her a slice of orange at an outdoor playground. She ended up crying in a tube slide.

She planned to seed her kids. And their friends at birthday parties.

A fourth led to a homeless man in Portland ME who, when the priestess handed him the orange whole, yelled so loud he burst Tone's right eardrum…from fifty feet away.

The priestess was virtually deaf for a week.

SOMEWHERE IN FLYOVER COUNTRY

"You know for every one person we stop," the priestess said as she read her Tarot cards, "Likely five are getting through and seeding."

Tone considered this as she kept working on the bike between rides. She had to steal all the parts in drips and drabs from all kinds of parts stores across the Midwest.

"I know," she said.

"Do we continue on? Can we stop it?"

"No," Tone-Bone said. "But I don't think winning is the point."

MOTEL BRAIN

The next flame was matte black. Hard to even see. They struggled to follow it. Lost it a few times. Had to relight. It led to a small town in southern Ohio. To a motel off a desolate back highway. Tone cut the engine and rolled to a stop. The matte black flame went straight to door number six. They watched from across the parking lot. It was noon. Blazing. Windless. A sky so blue it felt threatening in its beauty.

The flame did something none had done before. It passed *through* the door.

"What's that mean?" Tone said.

The priestess shrugged. "I can imagine nothing good."

The closest room was number one, on the far end of six. They tried the door. Locked. The front window was locked. But the back window was propped open with a wedge of two by four. They got in that way and found out why the window was cracked. It smelled like hot death in the motel room. Something at one time had either bled all over the carpet or their bowels broke open. Either way, it was foul. A spot in the carpet seemed to weep with a dark liquid when someone stepped on it. Tone-Bone took first watch at the small table with a gun in her lap, watching through the chintzy curtains across the courtyard and parking lot at room number six. Not that the gun could do much. But this black flame was starting to throw her off. Whatever was in room six was different than what they'd been chasing before.

The priestess yawned and lay on the bed by Tone.

"I'm not waking you up if something goes down," she said.

"You won't need to. I'll know about it before you do."

"What, you gonna feel it through your bare feet?"

But the priestess was already asleep.

Travelling together by motorcycle across the country had been rough.

Nothing much happened for the rest of the day. Some kids skateboarded through the parking lot as the sun went down, but they found nothing useful and left. The few rooms that were occupied, except room six, turned their side table lamps on as the sun went down. The motel vacancy light strobed on. Plenty of vacancy. A couple returned in a pick-up, got out, stumbled with good cheer to room number three, and almost fell into the room. Lots of laughing.

The priestess was still asleep at 12:35 AM. That's when room number six's door opened, and someone was pushed out. A younger guy with light hair and a medium build. He tripped on the door's threshold and fell to his knees. He didn't look scared so much as inconvenienced. But Tone-Bone knew he should be scared. She leaned in as close as she could and squinted. Her eyesight wasn't amazing. She *recognized* this guy. As he stood and brushed his jeans and shirt off, she placed him. The catering guy.

The guy that her friend Keller had brought to her cabin some years back. The guy who'd sort of started all this shit up. What was his name? Cale? Gage? Dane?

Cade. Right.

Now, he'd *already* been seeding people for Mr. Dinosaur. So what in the hell was she supposed to do about that?

Then another person exited the room and put a gun at Cade's back.

Poxy. Former lover. The Fanged Wonder. God. She looked good. Damn good. A cold, vampiric, calculating murderer—but attractive. What in the *hell* was she doing with this guy? Weren't they on the same side? Tone remembered that there weren't really any sides in their type of lives. Only crude networks of on-again and off-again alliances with a scattering of trust among them. Which wasn't wholly true. There was no trust. Every relationship she'd had was just a lit fuse. You could trust a fuse for as long as it was lit. When it was gone, you better be gone, too. That wasn't trust. That was survival.

"Hey, Betty Boop." Tone kicked the bed. "You got that Tarot deck with you? The one with the Yawning Dog and the Six of Shits?"

Without turning over, the priestess said: "Always, hun."

"I'm going to need a reading. The sooner the better."

"We got company, huh."

"Yeah."

Poxy pointed Cade in the reverse direction toward the main office. But then stopped. She'd instinctively opened her mouth a little and held it up with her head cocked. The way cats do when they get a strong scent.

"Don't move," Tone said.

Poxy pushed Cade down the walkway past room five, room four, room three—turn left—room two and then room one. Tone had crouched low behind the bed and aimed the gun at where Poxy's head would be if she kicked in the door. She wanted to believe Poxy could smell the shit and blood that soaked into her pants right then, as she knelt onto the carpet, but she knew Poxy could smell *her*. Wanted to taste *her*. Then *end* her.

Poxy sniffed at the door. Drew back. The nightshadow thrown by the parking lot lights showed them going back up the walkway.

Tone-Bone shook the priestess. "I thought you were all raring to go."

"I am. This is my defensive posture."

She sprung up and went to the small carryall by the TV. She pulled out a Tarot deck while Tone resumed her position at the table. Poxy was taking Cade *back* to room six? The door didn't close all the way.

This wasn't good.

The radiator by the bathroom hissed. No wonder it smelled like an elephant enclosure. The heat was on. This motel deserved to be burned to the ground.

The priestess shuffled her deck and dealt the cards. It was a split second reading. Rough. Imprecise.

"The Three of Tongues. The Sick Zephyr. And The Black Cancer."

"What does all that mean?"

The priestess clucked. "A dark change."

How vague.

Poxy shut the door behind her and proceeded back past room five, room four, room three.

Turn left.

And—

Wait. There was a spot where Tone lost sight of her and now she couldn't see her.

Shit shit shit

She'd spent years with this woman but watching her walk was like observing a hologram designed to confuse you. Or watching a copy of yourself get up out from your own body at the table and start doing chores around the house against your will. She didn't know that woman anymore. If she could rightly be called a woman. Poxy had transcended humanity into a gruesome species. Of what, Tone didn't know.

Five seconds of silence then a sound of something in the ceiling.

"You got the orange?" Tone said.

The priestess nodded. Tone-Bone turned from the window to check.

Tess bent to pick up her cards and Poxy was standing there.

She'd crawled through the bathroom window.

Tone fired a shot at Poxy's head, but she'd already leaned to shove the priestess into the wall by the beds. Whose body cratered a deep indentation in the drywall. She collapsed to the floor like a gnarled doll.

Poxy was faster than she'd ever been. And here Tone thought a gun would help.

"What are you doing, sister?" Poxy said. She shook her head in mock sadness. "Look how far you've come with that trailer trash shitbag. It's impressive but silly. I could smell you from fifty yards away. You stink good."

Tone fired two more shots. Both missed from five feet away.

Poxy leapt and pinned Tone to the floor. She devoured her smell and licked her neck and sucked her earlobes and kissed her with a wet, hot mouth. Tone fought at first. Then she kissed her back. Poxy's tongue tasted like old stamp glue. Slightly tangy and exciting. But not something you wanted in your gob for a long time. Poxy ground her pubic bone into Tone's. She wanted to mix as much sex and death as possible. And right as it seemed that they may just fuck right there on the floor, Poxy dove in and bit Tone-Bone's neck. And sucked.

But she didn't draw blood.

She pulled memories.

Poxy whispered into her ear. "Our god wants everything, Toney. *Everything*. Not like the Christians and their god who just wants your love. Ours, yours, needs every—single—thing. And it makes me feel g*ooo*d."

Tone knew right away the type of memory that Poxy wanted from her. The most *vulnerable* ones. Her life was unspooling backwards in front of her in flashy snippets. Prentiss, her dogs, the woman who gave her the name Tone-Bone. But the one Poxy worked so hard to pull was one of her father. Just before she stole the Scout. He'd been teaching her how to change the oil on it. He was confident and distant but loving and trusting. That was a somewhat nice image to rest on. Her father's trust right before she snatched it away from him. Though Tone never had that confirmed. Yet almost everything in her life flowed from that one spontaneous act of rebellion. An act that was underwritten by the absolute trust and love and confidence of her father—not to keep doing the same old shit day in, day out, but to be as independent and screwed-up as she wanted to be. If that memory was taken away, the question remained: *who or what would she be? Could she be who she was without it?* Or would she simply become one of a million Antonia Bonifaces? And if so, what did that mean?

A dark change, the priestess said.

A dark change, indeed.

So. There was more than one way for a vampire to take your life. Sure, blood. But memories? Tone had to appreciate the variation of corrupt weapons at hand. Poxy's saliva dribbled down her neck and it was cooling and oddly comforting. Poxy hooked on to that memory of her father and pulled. Pulled. Reeled it in. It was the domino that reversed all personality. And the memory seemed to clank and hiss as it left Tone's mind. *Hssssss.* The hissing grew stronger, louder. Warmer now instead of cooler.

"Heads up," the priestess said.

She was standing above both of them with a pipe torn from the radiator. Steam hissed and filled the room. The priestess swung down onto Poxy's skull and she collapsed off of Tone. Shreds of the memory remained. Enough to live off of. Enough, even, to maybe cultivate.

Poxy moaned and clutched her head. "Fucking bitch."

The priestess threw the pipe to Tone.

"That was for disemboweling me, you cunt."

Poxy wasn't without fight. She frantically canvassed the floor for whatever she could find and came upon a paper clip. A tiny inch and a half of metal, which, in one second, she'd straightened out enough to begin micro-stabbing Tess in the face with it at a blurring speed, pockmarks of bloody pimples appearing all over her cheeks and nose. Tess screamed and swatted.

Tone-Bone swung the pipe at both of Poxy's shins and broke them. In one fell swoop. Then she smashed Poxy's face. It was a belated and sad moment. But necessary.

"Wait," the priestess said. She got the orange and peeled it. Then she knelt by Poxy, who coughed blood and other vicious fluids, and worked on the fangs. She wiggled and tugged. Tone tapped the pipe on them and loosened them up. But they didn't kill her. The priestess cradled the fangs and spilled them onto the bathroom counter and took the stout water glass to crack the teeth. They split down the middle like tree nuts. She stowed an orange seed in each of them and then rubbed juice over them. The pieces bonded. It was like fantastical dental work. And satisfying. Tess reinserted the teeth. Tapping them in like ivory nails. And then she plucked a wire hanger from the closet hollow and unwound it. She bent the wire back and forth to snap it to sizes she desired and then jammed them into Poxy's mouth so as to create an impromptu orthodontic appliance. She wired Poxy's mouth shut. Crude but effective. The would-be vampire would be drinking her meals for the foreseeable future.

As she did this, Tone-Bone crossed the parking lot to room six and knocked on the door.

"Cade? Hello? McCall, where are you? You can come out."

The door swung open into an empty room. She checked everywhere. The guy had fled in the melee. Which was smart. Dumb but smart. She wasn't sure if she would've taken Cade alive or dead. Definitely would've made him eat some orange. But now she'd have to continue tracking him. Whether he was with yet another member of the Fuck-Offs and if that was better or worse, Tone couldn't decide.

A dark change, the priestess said. What would she decide that was? A turn from death to some form of life? Despair to hope? No. That was too clean. She hated clean. Maybe it was letting the priestess, Tess, into her life. Needing her now more than the other women she'd encountered. The priestess was her real sister now.

Tone-Bone stood in the half-shadowed room. Staring at the mussed comforter where Poxy must've sat with her captor.

The room phone rang. A big beige handset in a big beige cradle. She sat on the bed. Picked the phone up.

"Tone-Bone, the biker friend of Keller's," Cade said.

"Where are you."

"Not far. But listen, I'm sorry about what happened to your place. Your dogs."

That stung. A deep tornadic thrum was behind his voice. And static. He could've been on Neptune for all it mattered. Then an overlay as if someone with a deeper, firmer voice was talking behind him, at the same time. Speaking through him. Directing him. The dripping, acoustic necro-soaked voice. She knew who that was.

"Where are you," she repeated.

"Close but far enough away for it not to matter."

"This isn't going to end well for you."

Whooshing static. The crush of electrons, whizzing past each other somewhere in the ether. Space was a vacuum, Tone knew, but she swore she could hear a planet spinning. The grind of gravity on an eon of stone cruising through the emptiness.

And then with a true regret, he said: "It's not going to end at all."

The call was disconnected. Not even a dial tone.

She stared at the phone, hung it up, and went back to Room One.

They left Poxy splayed on the floor like a wrecked pictograph from a once-great civilization now lost. With her crude orthodontics and a newfound outlook on predatory life.

"What do you want to do?" the priestess asked.

Tone considered. She revved the motorcycle. "We need to find Cade. But it'll take a while. What are you thinking? Stay? Go?"

"I think I got the time, hun."

They hit up a dairy stand off the highway and got chili dogs and cheese fries and peanut butter milkshakes and felt the country air smother them with sweet grassy moisture. It was about the only time these two roughened semi-living bodies felt close to what some Midwesterners called *good livin'*. There was little doom in those milkshakes. And that worried them insofar as what they thought they had to carry as a burden was only subject to their imaginations.

Unfortunately, those were infinite.

They travelled by chaos. Backroads. Dirt paths. If they were on a lonely rural highway that ended in an odd number, they turned off on one with an even number. Or they went in a straight line one day. The next, they took every turn possible. They slept in fallow cornfields, wind breaks, old barns, dry drainage ditches, wildly large treehouses built by industrious fathers.

Tone-Bone only stopped for food or piss, crap, or sleep. The priestess didn't seem to really need any of those. Though Tone suspected she performed these human rituals *for* her to keep some semblance of a normal human ritual. To keep her steady for whatever final slab of atrocious shit was waiting for her on the other side of this wild flame chase.

Because at the end of the day, Tone knew we were all cultists of some form or another.

PAPER BAG

The kind of people you never want to live in a house in the woods are always the exact type who will live there. Including—Tone-Bone knew—herself. Call it TONE'S LAW.

They followed a flame deep along a two-lane blacktop that curved and dropped in the hummocky hills of some American middlespace. Everytown, USA.

There above this house's vent stack hovered the priestess's flames, a clutch of them like a confused flock of birds. The leaves on the trees around the house curled upward and had a black fringe to them. The air smelled of gasoline and fried foods. There were no curtains on the windows. Lights burned inside. She heard glasses clinking, the low mumble of conversation, someone politely laughing at a joke. Maybe it wasn't as desolate as she imagined out here—but then, what if she was walking into a situation where whackos were drinking kids' blood and praying over small piles of stones? Whatever. The flames above the house didn't lie. Whatever she had to deal with was in this house.

The thing Tess had talked about back at the Denny's. That Tarot reading.

This was it.

Tone tried Tess for support or instruction. But the priestess shrugged and said, "I'll be here. I'll be waiting. But I can't go in, hun."

"There's a gun in the saddlebag underneath the clothes."

"I don't need a gun, sweetie. But you need this."

She tossed the orange to her.

"Ain't that the truth," Tone said. It looked like the most normal orange ever grown.

She knew one thing as she pushed forward through the tall, uncut grass. One stone tablet-solid piece of knowledge handed down to her through some archaic part of her brain.

She knew she was going to kill whoever was in that house. Whatever was in that house.

No matter who it was. Or what it was.

They would be dead when she left. Or: she'd be dead. A hateful binary.

The orange had healed or repaired itself to new ripeness. She hefted it then stuck it into her jacket pocket. Standing on the welcome mat, she couldn't see anyone milling around. Must've been in another room, near the kitchen.

Tone didn't bother knocking. Went right in. The rank scent of human piss hit her. She had a hard time breathing through her nose—and yet she didn't really want to inhale the pissy air through her mouth and over her tongue, either. There were lots of lamps on. Small ones. Floor lamps. Novelty lamps. Tone-Bone got the feeling whoever lived here didn't want to be in the dark. Not even in the daytime. But she couldn't walk anywhere without stepping on open magazines—*People, Good Housekeeping, Rolling Stone, National Geographic*—every visible page had a face on it. There were at least 1,000 magazines open everywhere. The chatting and laughing was better located. It came from a turntable by the corner. Tone stepped on the magazines, tearing and crinkling the pages. Boot prints on the faces of this ventriloquizing party. She stopped in the middle of the room, trying to see if she could sense movement or another body in the house. The propped-up record sleeve said *Kneale's Endless Party! Authentic Sounds of Socialization for the Lonely.*

Well. That wasn't weird at all.

Tone-Bone lifted the needle on the record. The air thickened. As if she'd aggravated the magazines. Or the pictures themselves in the magazines.

She pulled the Bowie knife from her shin scabbard.

Her heart did its rare *thuh-thunk.*

Again, she listened. Silence. Not even the comforting creak of an old house settling. The living room led to the hallway where to the left was a kitchen and to the right were the bedrooms. She chose left and half of the kitchen was blocked from sight by an old Frigidaire. Magazines covered every open space on the floor. In here they were browner, foxed, moldy. *Saturday Evening Post, Photoplay, Argosy, Pantomime, Weird Tales.* All faces. Eyes staring at her. She'd rather have had the *Kneale's* record back on. Felt like it would appease the faces scattered on the floor and counter. But as she turned, a voice said: "Are you hungry?"

Tone squeezed the knife and leaned over past the fridge.

A woman sat at the kitchen table. Hands in lap. Unthreatening. So far. Likely crazy.

Or: obviously crazy.

The orange's flames led Tone-Bone here for a reason. This woman was, in a guess made with the churniest of guts, that Other Thing's Plan. The orange in her pocket would know what to do and when.

The woman was older, but when Tone got a look at her, they were probably the same age. But something about how this woman lived her life, how she dressed, made her seem decades older. A loose chignon, a knitted shawl, wrinkled knuckles, a golden tennis bracelet. Her glance was cast down, and it was dark, so Tone-Bone couldn't see her all that well. The one room in the house with no lights.

"Door was unlocked," Tone said. "Sorry to interrupt."

"You just missed them."

"Who?"

"My friends."

Tone-Bone felt that someone was watching her. But no one was in the hallway except magazines. She wanted to retch. This house was necrodynamic.

"Please sit, Antonia."

"How do you know my name?"

The woman adjusted the shawl over her shoulders.

"You should eat. I know you're hungry. You don't eat enough."

"I'm fine, thanks."

"You've never been fine."

"How do you know my name?"

Tone-Bone edged close to the table, the better to see the woman's face. Paper crinkled. She thought it was her boot on the magazines underfoot again. But this was a drier, brighter sound. More alive. It came from the counter behind the woman.

A brown paper bag. A plain bag crimped at the top—just the way her father used to fold her lunch for her before she fled all those years ago. Her psyche spasmed.

"Do you know how big the universe is, Antonia?" the woman said. "I never understood, still don't, really. But 'big' and 'large' and words of that nature don't work. We have no proper language to capture what's beyond our world. But trust me when I say it's big enough for all of us. Any of us. Every single one of us."

"Are you alone here?"

The woman laughed.

"Eat something," she said.

The paper bag shifted. Or Tone thought it did. Like something inside shifted. She pictured a bunch of apples. One of them sliding past the others to create a slight bulge on the side.

"I told you. Not hungry."

"Suit yourself," the woman said, head down.

"What's in the bag?"

"I sometimes think of what would've happened had I stolen father's motorcycle."

Tone felt a sliver of cold, like a chilled flint surgically placed under the skin. Those pinpricks stole up and down her ribcage.

"What's your name?" Tone asked.

The woman looked up into Tone's eyes and she didn't need to know the answer to the question. All but certain who was sitting here in this house.

The question wasn't *who* this was but *when* she was.

She stared at herself.

"That was the moment for us," the Other Antonia said. "Did this happen because you left or because I stayed? In any case, we were chosen. Are you sure you won't eat anything?"

Her face was forced, pained—as if she was, had been, sitting on a live grenade for months or years. But Tone knew she wasn't sitting *on* it. She was sitting *in front* of it. Whatever "bomb" in the bag that turned out to be.

The paper bag's wax shined in the little light that broke through from the living room, although the angle shouldn't have worked. The back of the Other Antonia was lit more than the front. The bag seemed to reflect light, but in reality, it actually was emanating from it. A green, sick light.

The Other Antonia was everything Tone-Bone would've never wanted to be.

Put together, tame, contained.

The paper bag was…yes, it was sweating. Like Tone's old couch, covered in a slime.

"What's with the magazines? The record?"

Her counterpart turned embarrassed. "It was my company."

"Was?"

"You turned the record off. And my guests are upset."

Tone-Bone checked one of the magazines. The face that once was ecstatic, pained with joy, now aimed its gaze outward at her in a direct and cold stare. They all had changed. They all scowled at Tone. The Other Antonia frowned. She speared at the split nailbed of one hand.

"You've been here a long time," Tone said.

The O.A. nodded. Now she leveled her gaze at Tone. Crying in slow, gluey drops.

This homebound version of Antonia explained that she led a life opposite to how the biker version had led. She'd worked at a nursing home. She'd cared for their father as he aged. Yes, for the Other Antonia, he returned from Europe and the Nazis. She never learned to love the motorcycle. Didn't want to. She didn't even learn about Tone-Bone (her other self) until some years ago when she received a phone call. She spoke with a man or a voice— because she couldn't sense a body this voice could've come from. It told her everything, showed her everything. Then, as she was on the phone, there was a knock at the door and the Other Antonia found a paper bag from which she pulled—yup, you guessed it— the impossible objects that Tone-Bone had to deliver to that Cade McCall. The voice on the phone—

"Mr. Dinosaur," Tone whispered to herself.

"Huh?"

"That's a name someone else gave it."

Something scraped across the concrete in the basement. They both heard it. Neither acknowledged it.

"A little silly, that name. But I guess it's appropriate. I've been in this seat for a long time and that voice has shown me things— history. Talked to me, *in* me. Did you know how the dinosaurs died out?"

"Boredom?"

The Other Antonia laughed. But it was more of a phlegmy gurgle. Tone-Bone noticed she'd peeled the nail off now. It was a wet red bed of soft pulpy flesh. She snorted and started on another nail. Tone leaned over to see where she tossed it. And there on the floor was a congealed keratinous pile of previously grown, torn off, and discarded fingernails.

"Sure you won't eat? Please *please*—" the O.A.'s voice became serrated and low, "—please please I just have one last treat to offer." The magazines at Tone's feet were snapping at her now, biting, flapping their pages, working their way (some of them) into proto-animal forms. *How much time did she have left in this house?*

"Uh, I've seemed to've lost my appetite—I thought those objects last forever?"

(Should she save her alternative self? she wondered. How? Where would they go? Could Tone-Bone stab her other self in the face if it came to it?)

"Some of the last bit I gave to father in the nursing home."

Little had churned sadness in Tone-Bone. There wasn't much after all these years. Maybe losing her dogs. Maybe reading *Pet Sematary.* But now the thought of her own self feeding that heavy cylinder or the perfectly black hole to her own father was mutilating her where she stood.

The top of the paper bag uncrinkled. Slowly so that each crease of the waxed paper echoed off every surface. The glow inside spread all over the room like a bright fog. The floor trembled. Tone-Bone knew that whatever was in the bag was also spread throughout the house and, almost certainly, in the basement. From the corners of her eyes, it seemed as if the outside was moving. Or the house was incrementally turning. She couldn't be sure of which.

"What do you want?" Tone-Bone asked.

"To get the fuck out of this house, what else?" The O.A. paused. Looked down, then back up. "To live *your* life."

"What do I get? Do I get a father?"

The Other Antonia said, "You will. You can." She scoffed. "As much as I ever did, anyway."

"What?"

"He left twice to fight the Germans. He said he'd leave me at the drop of a hat to fight fascism no matter what. Had to find my way without him for years."

There it was. She'd been tapping into the Other Antonia's mind at the restaurant. That daydream conversation she'd had. Feeling her feelings. Remembering her memories. They were sparking off each other in proximity. What the hell.

Tone-Bone wanted to tell the O.A. about the farm boy she killed—all the others. How her life wasn't an alternative salvation. Anyway, she didn't want to swap. The point wasn't to perpetuate life and sadness.

"Do you know what the dinosaur killer does? It eats you backwards. Eats everything that's been a part of your life until you're totally removed. I can see it coming for me. I've been kept on the hook in a way. Delayed."

The orange in Tone-Bone's pocket rang like a telephone— again. Again and again.

Speaking of delayed, Tone pulled the orange from her pocket, placed it on the table like a first grader for a strident teacher.

The record in the other room revolved and voices screamed. Deep voices mewling. Wailing. A medieval triptych converted into audio.

"Answer it!" the O.A. said. "Answer it, goddamn it!"

One didn't answer the orange. One cut it open. Tone-Bone slid the Bowie knife out and held it over the fruit as a judgment.

"Do it," the O.A. said.

She pressed the knife edge into the skin and felt the give of the mass. She sliced it. Juice bled. Rind flayed. The halves fell away and there was the absolute blackness inside. Void. Pure and totalizing. The kind of dark that had to only exist pre-galaxy. A form of reality that didn't acknowledge or recognize light as a wave or a particle or even as a concept. Thick yet depthless obliviating black.

The replicated version of herself sitting at the table didn't bother her. No, not in any way. It was the paper bag that bothered her. Yes. Because even though Tone-Bone felt like she'd been passed over by the unforgiving world and whatever lifehungry fiends pushed it forward at the oarlocks with their recriminating whims, she knew in the shell of her most interior self (that consisted of nerve endings) that she was still very much mortal. One heartbeat a day, an hour, whatever, or not. And a subversion had taken place within her during that debate in her house with the fat-slathered couch. A divorce had been signed between her and her former outlook on life. It was nothing so conscious or rational—just so much electrical clanging jarring her brain and memories and maybe even her other less-important organs. Thus, the paper bag held a hard lesson for her. She would have to open it further, wide enough to dip her hand into it.

The top edge of the bag rippled. The edges studded with tiny cilia.

Both women picked up an orange half. As they did, *something* leapt from the paper bag toward Tone-Bone and she brought up the knife in time to—

To what?

In time to be shown something. To have her head swallowed by a giant mouth formed from the bag's opening as she held the orange to her face. A final revelation before death perhaps.

In the orange and in the mouth of the paper bag, she witnessed the worst horror she could conceive of—the small horror of blind devotion. The horror of living *the wrong life*.

And in this case, a life devoted to her father and his needs.

In this other world: the Other Antonia never left.

She never stole the Indian 101, though she thought of it. She *desired* it. But the desire died in her unopened the way an insect captured by her would suffocate in an unventilated Ball jar. (Tone felt all this, wore all of O.A.'s emotions like a second skin that dug eternal channels into her body and psyche.) The motorcycle stayed parked in the detached garage like a sleeping beast under the oily canvas tarp. O.A. obsessed over the bike from afar but decided to never touch it for fear of what her father might do or say.

Instead, she allowed the girls at school to ask her to study groups and to the soda fountain for an egg cream. When she wore slacks, the girls scoffed or tsked. She debated. She wrestled with the pressure. She caved. She wore the skirts that would let her slide through society with no problem. But at home she wore denim dungarees or cotton slacks her father had forgotten about. He never explicitly forebade her the clothing (he was always worried she'd realize the self-sustaining power he knew she had in her) but made whispered, nearly inaudible, comments about boys not wanting to court another boy. This bothered her, of course. Not because she worried a silent shit about boys. Speaking of boys, they were disappearing into boot camps and men like her father were making the walls of life pinch on theirs like calipers. She took notice of the women. She'd always felt different toward women. She preferred their look, their shape, their smell. Too many of them were clueless about her desires—and like those sublimated desires for the motorcycle in the garage and the comfort of the jeans—her needs were necessarily plunged into the coldest, most remote, wastelands inside her mind. The O.A. fashioned this part of herself to be so forbidding as to make her own curiosity pull back in crude disinterest. (*Tone-Bone felt herself pulsating inside this other woman's life—smells of powder make-up and saddle soap, gasoline, oil, and hair tonic, the whip and crisp of air-drying laundry on the line, the sugary sting of cherry flavoring and Moxie—and she actively fought against it. To escape entrapment. Yet still having to obey in the pseudo-existence the arcing and dutiful obligation to act and talk and think a certain way. She hated the mere thought that she could've ended up this way, and while she was frustrated and sad, she didn't know why the O.A. was forcing her—*OR WAS SHE? WHO WAS CONTROLLING THIS?*—to re-live or pre-live all of this socially obedient bullshit. Tone-Bone still could feel the Bowie knife grip in her hand in the real world thrusting up toward whatever had lunged at her from the paper bag.*)

The O.A. waved goodbye to her father as he left for his own stint in the Army doing his part to fight Hitler and fascism. She was legally watched by an aunt. He'd been pacing like a dog on Benzedrine in the months leading up to his getting the nod from the service. The sergeant he talked to said he was almost too old. Her father said age don't matter to a Nazi. True enough. He knew they were going to take him. The O.A. didn't want him to go and she hoped they'd see he was a widower with a young girl. Because after he left, who would be the plug in the drain of her desires? With him gone, she'd give in to everything. But was that so bad? *The sweaty cottony smell of a girl's foot after being in a shoe all day. Sitting among a group of girls in a chilly movie theatre.* The O.A. wanted to say no, (*Tone yelled NO!*), but again, a life of regret is built up of innocent thoughtless decisions, small rejections of the self—choices that deflated and skinned the deepest, most fulfilling wants and flaring lights of the mind's eye. Once all those decisions build up into a shiny carapace of self-abnegation, then the transformation would be complete. *Was* complete. She'd turned her desires into an armored yet defenseless insect that suffocated slowly at the bottom of the glass jar of her life—a clear boundary that was fragile yet eerily strong and too complicated for her to break. (*And really now Tone-Bone too would stare at the sealed and falsely bright ceiling of her alternative life, thinking, Could it have been different? And if so, when? How? These questions arriving entirely too late for her in this world, but maybe, just maybe, not too late in the other.*) She went to teacher's college and taught teenagers. And she tried to do something radical with her life, but all she could do was kiss another woman who taught at a different high school. Another woman who *wanted* that kiss in the teacher's lounge after classes were over, the rough wool plaid of their skirts rustling against each other, blouse buttons catching on each other as their chests touched, and an elbow knocking a ceramic coffee mug into the sink. She was married, this other woman, but clearly interested, and after the kiss, which made them both sweat, a lock of disdain and brutal banishment clamped down, as if the O.A. had tricked her into being attracted to women, when in reality, it was simply this other teacher's desires being boldly manifested. The choice was breaching forth. Choose what you want and live more than ever. Or choose to reject all this and be convenient and push it all away. The O.A. knew in her liver, in her red blood cells, that what scared people more than monsters or death was *total and true change.* Necessary mutation. But the thought of all that, that such a mutation was required, was equivalent to the Creature from the Black Lagoon crawling out of your toilet while you had your soft, vulnerable ass cheeks exposed over the musty bowl of water.

But not *this* Antonia Boniface. Not Tone-Bone. She didn't feel that way.

Tone-Bone pulled on mutation like an anchor from the bottom of swampy water.

She wanted to reel up the creature. She willingly planted her vulnerable ass *into* the Black Lagoon.

She wanted to tell the teacher who locked eyes with the O.A. in lust and longing that there was no hell so red as the one you manufactured for yourself everyday under the guise of behaving *appropriately*.

And the O.A. gleaned this in drips and drabs. That hell was all around you all the time. Like when she spent time with women from the school or the local cribbage club and caught them from the corner of her eye while she stood at a counter mixing a G&T or a bloody Mary, their hair curled and their necks sprayed, smelling like L'Interdit or Chanel N° 5 or Hermes but their faces creased and gray and eyeless with hooked teeth as chapless ghouls carved in granite. And then the Other Antonia would look directly at her friends and see nothing but smiling Grace Kelly acolytes. The hell that was hidden in the peripheral vision.

The O.A. was surrounded by this hell of her own making— or was it Tone-Bone's making by her initial fleeing?—when she noticed small disfigurements of reality. She'd walk into a room in the library to pull a book or into a restaurant for a meal and catch everyone looking at her. *Staring* at her. And all the eyes were square-shaped or their faces were similarly warped because they were actually sitting somewhere else in another galaxy and just their astral projections were visible. She never knew for sure. Because a moment later, the eyes and faces were normal.

"And then, you know what happened, Antonia, don't you?" the O.A.'s voice said from far away.

Tone-Bone listened. She watched.

"Hell develops. It progresses."

The Other Antonia was now taking care of her father, this father who didn't die in World War II. The Indian 101 Scout rusting and ignored in the garage. The O.A. now smells like Givenchy and hamburger grease on any given day. She wears firetruck red lipstick and hates it. She reads women's magazines not for the recipes but because she masturbates to the pictures.

Hell develops.

Clearing the father's trach tube and moistening his mouth with a wet rag and wiping his ass and emptying his catheter bag. Smearing ointment on his lesions and reading *Stars and Stripes* to him every so often. The painful smell of physical stasis and malingering and noisome medicinal fogs.

And then one day in the midst of this toxic bubble, the phone rang.

The O.A. answered it.

Who was on the other end?

The Guest, Tone-Bone thought.

Mr. Dinosaur. You know it.

Inside this shared dream of the O.A.'s, Tone-Bone felt the orange flex. It wanted a word in edgewise. But not yet. *No. Wait. Patience.*

"That's exactly who it was," the O.A. said.

And it wanted to help her, it said.

It said it knew what she was going through and that it could help her.

So she asked how—and her father aspirated then. Choking that almost resembled a cackle. She held the phone in the crook of her neck as she tried to grope for the plastic bulb to suck the trapped saliva out. But the O.A.'s father was dying. He couldn't breathe. And not from the spit. His neck swelled and the veins there bulged. He went cyanotic and fast. Lips tremoring. Eyes rolling outward. And a chilled sweat coating him like greasepaint. While this cobalt-cold voice on the other end of the phone breathed crushed particles at her.

Antonia, it said. You are not listening to me.

"I am," she said. Now she used a finger to prod around in her father's mouth, scooping out thick foamed mucus. It came from nowhere.

No, you are not, it said.

"I am!"

Her father's mouth spat her finger out along with a gout of muddy-colored bile and digestive juices. The jaw was pulled down by an unseen force and the tongue slipped down. She'd thought he died.

But the phone's voice came out from his mouth and brushed past her neck and face.

NO YOU ARE NOT.

She threw the phone's handset at her father's head in a disgust reflex. Left a deep dent above his eyebrow ridge. It should've bled but didn't.

The thing's voice—the voice from nowhere—crept from her father's mouth now. Told her that she could have a different life, a life she always wanted, a life currently being lived by Tone-Bone. That life that was due her, the life *stolen* from her. Mr. Dinosaur explained what Tone-Bone and the Fuck Offs had done, summoning it. But they were neglecting their end of the bargain.

"I'll do it," the O.A. said. "Whatever it is, I'll do it. Just get me out of here."

DONE.

And her old man, their father, relented and died. For Tone-Bone, seeing this was a trauma she hadn't expected to experience. She'd manufactured deaths for her father through sheer will as a way toward closure—though that word, *closure*, wasn't the kind of thing that Tone went in for. There was no closure. There was only the end. And it came when it came. So fucking deal with it. But this, this paralyzed drama she was forced to endure, whether real for her in her universe and reality or not, didn't matter. It was her father suffering and dying. Even after dying, the body proceeded to leak and vomit up small pieces of ephemera. Objects. The first small strange, impossible things. And, finally, something large. Whatever it was pushed its way up in a reverse peristalsis. Her father's neck working and constricting and expanding like the body of a python swallowing a whole goat. The Other Antonia wanted to feel rage and disgust. The object widened his esophagus. A horrible gas lurched out. The smell of the body's internal moist spaces and the already decaying cells of his corpse. Blood sprayed up into the O.A.'s face. She tasted the warm saltiness of her father's lifeblood. The object was slicing her father's soft palate flesh in half as it emerged. The delicate paper flesh of her elderly father's face. His upper jaw. His yellowed teeth. It was a knife. The blade forced a path up and through in a crescent. It was all but cutting his head in two. But the knife was the final necessity of her escape plan. All these years a prisoner. Her father could take a knife to the face for her, just this once. Just this once for his loving daughter, without doing anything, knowing anything, she *knew* she had to feed people the strange objects and pieces that spewed forth from him. And that before long this Mr. Dinosaur would eat her papa. So she left him there. She moved on to live, to find the life she deserved.

At this point, Tone could feel the O.A. wrapping herself around her life. Licking the sides of it and tasting the history and the vivacity. Plugging the holes in memory with her own. Sniffing at the nostalgia as if it was an aroused crotch.

Another escape from Fuck Mountain.

Tone-Bone was spit out by the paper bag into this shared reality with the Other Antonia. Tone held the Bowie knife in hand. Once freed and back in the kitchen, she moved instinctively, as a child does when stung by a bee.

The blade lodged firmly in the O.A.'s face. Through the left cheek and, Tone thought, what felt like the meat of the tongue. There was no blood. Her doppelgänger was just as she was—without a heartbeat or life in the normal way.

"In a way, I'm sorry," Tone-Bone said. "But not too much."

The O.A. moaned a response. Hard to parse.

"We never had a brother or a sister. So this does feel like a special moment."

Blood drooled from the wound in the O.A.'s cheek and down the slope of the knife, curling along the serrated edges of the Bowie. It dripped onto the table in loud splats.

"Your life ate shit. I see that now. And for *that* I'm sorry. But I can't let you take my life and swap with yours like a fan belt. Nuh-uh. Anyway, you wouldn't know what to do with my life, with me—you're not built for it."

Tone-Bone wondered if it was too late already. Had the O.A. done the damage? Someone squeezed tight enough on her that the switch had been completed? Was walking into this house the tripwire? Was the paper bag swallowing them up enough? Or was maybe leaving the trigger? Who knew. Nothing could be trusted. Not even her gut anymore.

Through the knife, her mirror-image said: "EEEee Arrrre!"

"No, we're not. That way is hell, too. Don't you get it? There's only hell. There's only the darkness of your own fucked choices." Still, the tightness that her Other had on her—soul?— was invariably tight. Constricting. Possessive.

The O.A. was weeping. The paper bag was now under duress and desiccating and spasming in some alien deaththroes. The basement rumbled underneath. Ill light shot from the heating registers in the floor.

Tone could see something moving in the basement. Wide shadows. But there was no time to predict. The floor burst open like and spewed forth a creature of indeterminable size. As it emerged, the O.A. was impaled by a long shard that poked out of the creature's skin. The O.A. now was oddly a part of it. Moving and sliding in the tiny kitchen. Tone-Bone pressed back against the wall. She could see the end of it now deep in the ceiling corner. A wolf-headed snake with rotten gray scales and skin. It had five eyes and six small skeletal-like arms bursting from the side of the head. It was one of these that had pierced the O.A. She flailed like a blood puppet on strings made of tendons. Tone squeezed both halves of the orange into her mouth and the juice ran down her chin. It burned. She took off to the right, out the kitchen, down the hallway, and up the stairs. She pushed herself. She dodged left into a slant roofed bedroom with a dormer. The wolfsnake glided up the stairs, breaking plaster off walls and busting balustrades. Its head crashed through the hallway ceiling. Tone-Bone ran at the window with the knife in her hand and burst through as the wolfsnake rushed to where she stood. She landed on the lower roof. She lay there for one second too long and the horror pushed its head out the window and snapped at her with reflective fangs. The eyes mirrored one million different Antonia Bonifaces and Tone saw them all—and all of them were not her, even though they shared her DNA, physiology, and habits. She knew the intent. If this would subsume her, she would be thrown into one of the one million lives and forced to eternally recur through them. Thus, her hell was herself, forever, with no escape. (The eyes swirled a moment like an oily glaze sliding over them and they began to blink in a hypnotic succession such that Tone-Bone wanted to relent against the wolfsnake—she, in a way now, could see in those eyes of oil and eternity a kind of retreat. She reached out a hand. Her own hand which now seemed so fragile and spotted. Frequently broken. Pained. Maybe getting arthritic. Wouldn't it be better, wouldn't it be a relief to be in another, younger body forever and ever, over and over, as opposed to this one? Wasn't that true freedom?)

Instead, she stabbed the middle eye. The horror wailed and the tail of it inside slung around like a wrecking ball using the O.A. as the weighted end now. Tone felt in her pocket and dug her fingers into the split orange like it was her own wound on the side of her body. She jammed the juice-slicked fingers into the entity's suppurating eyehole and the gore sizzled with it. A banshee's scream pealed out across the woods. The gore bubbled and foamed and small wriggling worm-like tubes poured forth and onto the roof. Tone smashed them or brushed them off. The horror pulled hard backwards. Down to the basement, she figured. The O.A. lolled behind with a tired and desperate look on her face.

Tone-Bone had to split. Like, five minutes ago. She crawled back in and returned to the kitchen where there was a massive hole in the floor. The O.A. lay teetering on the edge, a series of puncture wounds along her side like shoelace holes in a sneaker. Tone searched the scattered and slimy vomitus on the table and found a small pyramidal shape. She tried to scoop it up, but it was much heavier than it looked. The size of a cigarette butt at most. She heaved it up with one hand with all the strength she had left. Pulled the knife from the O.A.'s face. She pointed the bloody point a quarter inch from the right eyeball.

"Open," Tone said.

Her other half grunted. Shook her head.

There was no forgiveness in Tone-Bone. Not yet.

"*Open!*"

The O.A. opened reluctantly as if more worried about the consequences from whatever entity carried more probity than the hardcore biker version of herself. Tone lugged the impossible object into the other's mouth and immediately the head was thrown back and the hands went to her throat in distress. Despite this, the O.A.'s clutch on Tone was solid. Almost choking. There was a race to death. But even in death, what did a win look like? Suffering more than the other? Was it just enough to have nerve endings over sensory oblivion? Was that what we were all clamoring for? *More pain, please. Anything but relief from suffering.* The O.A. swallowed the object as fast as she could.

Screaming, agony came from the living room. The magazines. Everything in the house sensed The End. The end of something, anyway. It was on its way. The house was coming unglued from the moorings, the foundation. Pipes burst throughout. Tone-Bone smelled sewage and natural gas. The O.A. smelled it, too.

The hissing like a vaporous, combustible snake.

The O.A. pulled herself up with an impressive amount of willpower. She reached up and opened a drawer. The O.A. frantically searched for something inside. A gun? A knife?

No.

A book of matches.

(just like the Nazi's house—we think exactly alike, then)

She flipped it open and tried to light one at a time letting them burn all the way down. The timer was started, then.

Tone ran. But in the living room the magazines fluttered up like manic birds and in that precise angle that we've all experienced, they cut her, her skin, on the face, hands, neck. Especially the neck. *(she doesn't care if I live because she wants to take both of us out of the picture because if she can't have my life no one could).* They wanted that jugular. It was like an attack of fanged bees. Tone-Bone slashed her way to the door, but the thought occurred that one *could—CAN—*die from a thousand cuts. As she touched the doorhandle, she realized that they might not be able to kill her but the pull of annihilation was still strong. And what was the point of living if you weren't in your own life? She sliced through a solid formation of paper like a vast living wall. Then she was through to the outside. The door slammed behind her.

Shrieks of desperation.

She ran as fast as possible making sure the orange was protected. Her arms were sleeved in her own blood. She tripped on a gopher hole and as she hit the ground, the house in the woods exploded. Shards of framing fell on her. A brick landed on her thigh. Bits of burning paper rained down on her as she stumbled to the bike where Tess was crouched and hiding. "Bit of a let down, huh?" she said. Tone tried to kick the bike awake. It was dead as dicks. So they watched the Other Antonia Boniface's house burn and melt and crumble into a charred stain on the earth. She thought she could make out the shimmering outline of a seated skeleton at a nonexistent table. But that was demented desires of revenge.

Tone pushed the bike. They walked it as far as they could along the country road until she either fell over or bled out. When she next woke, she was lying in yet another stand of pines off the road and a fine mist fell from a colorless sky. The priestess was beside her the whole time humming some ancient tune from a time before stringed instruments.

FULL OF BLOOD

Tone-Bone was fleeing herself on her own bike.

The sky was the color of bourbon dotted with blood drops. They had arrived somewhere in East Tennessee. Somewhere with kudzu hanging off of everything manmade construct.

They had been riding nonstop for days. The chill of what had happened still on their skin like an unshakable frost. Slowly, but not all at once, the parallel muscular grip of the Other Antonia dissolved like lard in a hot pail.

Expect nothing good, though. That was the motto.

Tone-Bone passed a low building surrounded with bikes. Choppers. Pick-ups. The smell of charred flesh. Maybe animal. She was hungry and told the priestess they were getting grub. The priestess still hadn't found or worn any proper shoes. She mentioned this lack of footwear.

"No shirt, no shoes, no service."

Tone turned around, pulled in, and cut the engine. "Well, if they got a problem, lose the shirt. I bet they'll serve you then."

There was a young man outside leaning against a concrete parking pole who was a dead ringer for the farm boy she'd killed as a teenager. He only stared at her while he picked a bloody scab on his neck.

As soon as they walked in, she knew it was a mistake. Or a cockeyed blessing.

A dark change.

She'd quit paying attention to license plates weeks back. The bar was full of leather-denim men with an identikit mix of facial hair. A mix of anarchic trolls and kobolds smoking Marlboros and holding two beer bottles. No one gave the women a nod or the merest notice. The pool hall lights above the tables fought to cut the fug of cigarette smoke like a gelatinous solid. It was the light of mad scientist laboratories and serial killer basements. Some dark metal played on a stereo out of sight. Porno played on a small color TV duct-taped to a jerry-rigged platform on a wall. Centerfolds of spread open vulvas thumbtacked to the wall behind the bar where a bartender was eyefucking the priestess—that otherworldly creature who moonlighted as a seductive cornfed harlot but would just as soon suck the eyeballs from your orbital sockets.

Tone-Bone approached the bar and ordered two beers. The bartender didn't say shit about the priestess's bare feet. Next to the vulvas was a flier for a white nationalist romp that night. Tone thought she heard German then. Mixed in the muddle of phlegmy voices. And the smell of those foreign cigarettes the Nazi used to smoke. She turned to observe these beasts in their habitat.

There.

The hand sign that they used to give each other. She saw it. Like the one she saw the young skinheads give way back in

Indiana. And another one…*there.*

She asked the bartender about the romp. Where was it? Who ran it?

He tried not to act surprised at the question. At a farm nearby. He didn't really know.

"But you gotta have the entrance fee," he said.

"Which is what."

"A passphrase."

"Give it to me."

The bartender considered her. He shook his head.

"Aren't you someone's old lady? I seen you around here."

"I'm a Fuck-Off."

The man snorted. "That's a made-up pussy group, man. You ain't no Fuck-Off. That's a bedtime story."

From inside her jacket she pulled out the patch she ripped from her jacket with the zombie'd middle finger.

He shrugged.

"Give me the phrase," she said.

"Drink your beer and get fucked."

"Give me the phrase or I'll break your face."

The bartender laughed. She didn't. He coughed.

"Orange juice," he said. "The phrase is 'orange juice.'"

"No shit?" She shook her head and enjoyed the good vibrations pinging through her limbs.

The priestess sensed what was up. She didn't drink beer, so she pushed it to Tone who downed it. Then she leaned in and whispered something to Tess, who nodded and went outside.

And like an internal alarm had gone off, a door in back opened and the tallest biker she'd ever seen with the longest beard yelled, "Aye-o," and wolf-whistled. Like automatons, the entire assembly of bikers stood and moved into that area and the door shut behind them. Only one elderly fella was left in the corner, nursing a boilermaker.

"What is it, naptime?" she said.

The bartender said it was a meeting. And none of her business.

In that moment, she felt another version of herself split off—probably to go live a normal life—and Tone wished that version well—but she was committed to this one.

The priestess returned as Tone slid off the barstool. She handed Tone the radiator pipe she'd broken off at the motel and brought with her. Tone-Bone mentioned a final thing to the priestess, who then went into the bathroom. Tone hefted the pipe. The bartender hadn't noticed yet. Not until she started swinging at the empties on the bar. At glasses on the tables. Shotglasses. At the pool hall lights.

"You crazy bitch!"

She stepped onto the bar and smashed the TV. She jumped down and wiped out the barback and shelves of liquor. She swung extra hard and shattered the bar mirror. The metal on the stereo masked the shatter. When she got down, the bartender was reaching for a weapon under the bar. A pistol or a shotgun, Tone didn't know. Didn't matter. She swung the pipe at his stomach, and he doubled over. When he stood he called out "Elroy!" but Elroy didn't get the rest of the message. The bartender didn't even have time to get the last word out of his mouth.

Tone-Bone leapt and headbutted him.

Nose smashed.

Face cracked.

Blood splurting down like a busted soda machine.

She broke his skull good.

One of many skulls she'd break that evening.

Some bloated biker dunce walked in from the gravel parking lot, shocked and laughing from fear. His hands were smeared in something red and glistening but not from himself. He opened the bathroom door to wash it off and Tess barreled past holding all the soap she could find. She began to squeeze it all over the floor. Tone threw another bottle of dishsoap from behind the bar. They covered as much of that small place with soap and broken glass. Then Tone lit the liquor on fire.

Yeeeaaah.

Old Elroy in the corner watched all this with faded circumspection, as if he'd assumed that one day a terror would rain down upon them not unlike the events that were unraveling.

The bloated biker burst from the bathroom screaming because the red wouldn't come off and now it was in his beard and all over his face. His pure white patches with runic symbols and Gothic script were ocher and ruddled. Some permanent stain upon his being. But he was cut off to silence by the sight of flames crawling all over the bar. He yelled "fire", but it came out *fahr fahr fahr!* And when he tried to run to warn the others in back—he slipped on the soapy floor and onto a bed of broken glass. A shard of a bottleneck right in the kidneys.

Tone-Bone and the priestess stood guard at the exit to make sure no one left.

The priestess's feet were still somehow delicate in all that gore.

When the first few bikers burst from the back, Tone felt a thrill that she hadn't had since she'd stolen her father's motorcycle as a girl. She tried to hold onto that feeling, that memory for as long as she could.

She wasn't worried. She'd find McCall. The rest of her gang. All of them.

Besides, she had time. Her heart had bought her even more years. And no one was leaving this bar.

The men wouldn't be able to go anywhere. Tone-Bone knew that. Their motorcycles wouldn't start. No matter how hard they kicked. Thanks to Tess.

The engines were full of blood.

KYLE WINKLER lives in northeast Ohio with his family. He teaches college composition and rhetoric.

www.ingramcontent.com/pod-product-compliance
Lightning Source LLC
Chambersburg PA
CBHW012144140726
47991CB00009B/3151